PLANET OF THE ORCS

NOVEL I

WRITTEN BY
HIMATARO ZUKUNASHI

Airship

Seven Seas Entertainment

Shirono Mao to Kurono Eiyu vol. 1
© 2019 Himataro Zukunashi. All rights reserved.
First published in Japan in 2019 by Kodansha Ltd., Tokyo.
Publication rights for this English edition
arranged through Kodansha Ltd., Tokyo.

Seven Seas press and purchase enquiries can be sent to
Marketing Manager Lianne Sentar at press@gomanga.com.
Information regarding the distribution and purchase of
digital editions is available from Digital Manager CK Russell
at digital@gomanga.com.

Seven Seas and the Seven Seas logo are trademarks of
Seven Seas Entertainment. All rights reserved.

Follow Seven Seas Entertainment online at
sevenseasentertainment.com.

TRANSLATION: Roy Nukia
ADAPTATION: Linda Lombardi
COVER DESIGN: Nicky Lim
INTERIOR LAYOUT & DESIGN: Clay Gardner
PROOFREADER: Meg van Huygen, Jade Gardner
LIGHT NOVEL EDITOR: T. Anne
PREPRESS TECHNICIAN: Rhiannon Rasmussen-Silverstein
PRODUCTION MANAGER: Lissa Pattillo
MANAGING EDITOR: Julie Davis
ASSOCIATE PUBLISHER: Adam Arnold
PUBLISHER: Jason DeAngelis

ISBN: 978-1-64827-608-8
Printed in Canada
First Printing: October 2021
10 9 8 7 6 5 4 3 2 1

CONTENTS

CHAPTER I

HUMANITY DEFEATED

THE ORCISH LEGIONS had taken their positions atop the hill. Each stalwart soldier brandished a spear several times his own height, and their close-knit formation that extended far over the long ridge filled the autumn sky with the gleam of pointed blades.

Following the beat of a drum, a number of strangely dressed orcs approached the front of the formation in a mad dance. Shamans, perhaps. Most likely, this was how they bestowed courage and blessings upon their soldiers.

It had been a mere week since I was summoned to this world, and I was already set to challenge the enemy army.

The orcs looked little different from those I'd seen in other worlds. They were small, about chest height to an average human, but solidly built. Their fearsome faces looked like some freakish cross between a monkey and a pig, with drool dribbling down the tusks that protruded from their lower jaws.

According to the priests who had summoned me, orcs were a foul race birthed into the world by an evil god. They told me,

"An orc is about as intelligent as a dog and falls a little short of humans in speed and power. Duking it out one-on-one with sticks, even a common farmhand would come out the victor."

And apparently that was it—just like other orcs I knew of. However, they reproduced at a fearsome speed, so they were slowly overwhelming humanity by sheer force of numbers.

Still, there are plenty of ways to deal with a foe that can boast of nothing but numbers. As a veteran who'd saved twelve worlds already, I was sure that this would be a cinch.

I hummed a merry tune as the black-clad army took its position across the field. They totaled around ten thousand, give or take. This didn't trouble me; in fact, there were fewer of them than I had anticipated. Rather, the issue was that their movements were highly unified. They were clearly an *army*.

This was the opposite of what I'd been told to expect. We were supposed to be fighting a horde of beasts no smarter than dogs, whose only advantage was pure numbers—small fry easily dispersed with my hero's powers. Could it be that they were unified under that so-called evil god? I'd gotten the impression that he was a myth, not an actual threat.

Still, it was a foreign world. There was nothing unusual about gods being real—I'd killed a few in my day. That said, if there was some mysterious entity out there who was able to manipulate so many individuals, no doubt they must boast fearsome power.

It was starting to look like my duty in this world was to defeat that being. A harsh trial, yes, but not an impossible one. It's actually easiest when my heroic duty is laid out plain and simple.

"Finally found you." Sir Rigel, dressed head to toe in heavy plate armor, drew his horse near. He was captain of the dragon riders and boasted the title Lord of the Silver Blade, but today, of all days, he carried not his prized silver sword but an incredibly mundane piece of steel.

Once his horse was lined up next to mine, he apologized for the discourtesy of not lifting his visor to address me. "After all, it's quite a pain to contain my beard."

Sir Rigel was exceedingly religious. Ever since he lost his son, who was a fellow dragon rider, he had clung firmly to his god's teachings, which forbade putting a razor to his face. It was due to his faith that he supported me, the supposed Hero sent by God, before anyone else did. He'd even taken on a sort of caretaker role. In fact, he was the one who had afforded me my equipment and horse for this campaign.

Gaining the support of someone so influential this early on was definitely a promising sign. In the worlds I'd been summoned to before, I'd met people who didn't trust me in the slightest— even sometimes the very people who brought me there. I could hardly count how often I'd been sent off to fight some demon lord without proper backing.

"The battle will begin soon. Please return to camp."

Sir Rigel urged me to turn to watch the allied forces of humanity taking shape. My first glance wasn't entirely reassuring.

They were making a huge ruckus about how someone was stationed a little farther ahead last time and about how someone couldn't stand having certain other someones lined up right beside them. An argument over whether someone had bumped someone else with a shield was quickly escalating into a duel.

A plethora of different crests adorned the banners over their heads. There had to be over a hundred. Beneath them clamored the knights clad in lamellar armor, which is made of joined metal strips. The crests on their shields were even more varied than their flags.

Our forces boasted three thousand five hundred cavalry. Incidentally, the *horses* here were quite a lot larger, heavier, and firmer than the ones in my world, and each had a pair of sharp horns growing from its head. I thought they looked more like bulls. Protected by an apron-like piece of armor in front, they could make full use of their astounding leg strength to make a mighty charge.

Nearly all the knights straddling these steeds wore a helmet in the shape of the head of a beast. They resembled a devil's legions more than an order of justice. Either way, they certainly looked impressively strong.

We had roughly an equal number of foot soldiers behind the cavalry. They remained on standby in uneven formations. Their armor consisted of whatever they could get their hands on, while their weapons ranged from halberds to spears, from axes to swords, from bows to crossbows, and even included some grass sickles and pot lids. They were a mishmash of attendants, mercenaries, and conscripted farmhands, likely not the most reliable people to have on your side in a fight. For what it was worth, they had at least been divided between those with projectiles and those without.

We were trotting through a gap in the formation when I asked Rigel, "The enemy is quite numerous. Will we be all right?"

"Our numbers are nothing to scoff at either. Normally, there would be nothing to be concerned about, but..." The old man fell silent for a moment, clearly worried.

I urged him to continue with a glance.

"I presume those are just a diversion. Their main forces must be concealed behind the hills."

"The priests told me that orcs are just beasts without intellect."

"They become incredibly shrewd when it comes to war, and war alone. Take care not to take the priests' words to heart, lest they catch you off guard."

I didn't expect Sir Rigel to be critical of the temple. We hadn't known each other long, but I had never seen him skip a prayer before a meal. Whenever a sacred word passed his lips, his expression was the epitome of seriousness.

"I didn't expect to hear that from you," I said.

"It is not the priests I pray to."

I see.

Sending scouts would be our best bet to confirm his suspicions. However, there was forest to the right of the hill and wetlands to the left. That limited our chance of getting a good visual.

"We'd be able to immediately spot an ambush if we had our dragons," Rigel mumbled, frustrated.

Apparently, not long before I was summoned, the dragons entered their breeding season, which came once every few decades. During that period, every able dragon would gather at the Dragon Peak. Right now, they were probably all doing their best to find a mate. And thanks to that, the dragon riders who Rigel was so proud of had been reduced to mere horsemen.

That said, they were not going to expend their valuable dragon riders as if they were the common cavalry. The dragon riders were stationed at the main camp to guard the priests who would carry out the rites of war.

"But after we've gathered all the lords and their armies, we'll disgrace the princess if we return without engaging in a single battle."

The princess he spoke of was Princess Liana, the supreme commander of this operation. She was also called the Princess Knight. While she was young and seemed popular among the lords, I'd learned that strained class relations were found in every world.

My thoughts were interrupted by the loud bellow of a horn.

"Looks like the preparations are complete."

We spurred our horses the rest of the way.

◈

From behind us came the voices of over a thousand priests. Their chanting carried a peculiar modulation, resounding far and wide across the battlefield like a hymn. In concert with the intensifying sound, the insignia at their feet began to give off a blue glow. According to Sir Rigel, this ceremony delivered mana to the charms fastened to the knights' shields. Once activated, these would deploy a barrier against projectiles in a one-meter radius around us.

Eventually, the incantation shifted to a low murmur. The barriers were complete, and now a new chant was needed to maintain them. A horn blew loudly to announce that the preparations were ready, and a chorus of additional horns sounded in response.

Dividing into left flank, right flank, and center, the armies of allied lords began their advance, with the foot soldiers chaotically following behind.

The Knights Templar who I would be accompanying had yet to make a move. They were seen as one of the strongest forces in the kingdom, right up there with the dragon riders, and would charge in under the direct lead of Princess Liana once the opportunity presented itself.

As the air quivered with the earth-shattering pounding of hooves, the orcish legions made their move in kind. I saw the orcs positioned at the front of their forces holding gun-like objects.

No. They aren't gun-like. They are guns.

One of them—perhaps fumbling, or perhaps driven by fear—fired before the order was given. A flash of light and a long column of white smoke vomited out from the muzzle. The spectacle sent shivers down my spine.

Something in front of one of our vanguard emitted a faint glow, then a shrill clang. The bullet had been deflected by the magic barrier. Incited by the first shot, the orcish guns began bursting to life, scattering shots here and there until finally, the entire front line was enveloped in billowing white smoke.

Yet the unorganized barrage failed to inflict any damage on the knights. From the gaps in the smoke, I could see the orcs fleeing behind their line of spears after they fired, quickly replaced by new troops with loaded guns.

The horn sounded again, and the knights picked up speed. The hoofbeats making the earth shudder grew louder still.

They were almost halfway up the hill when the orcs let off their second volley in unison. The guns rang out, followed by a shrill grating sound as bullet clashed with barrier. Light burst where the bullets struck, and in the midst of the spray, the barrier lit up in a ribbon from end to end.

In a few places where the light was strongest, several knights toppled from their horses. It looked like a burst of light was produced when the barrier crumbled. I could hear the chanting of the priests behind me becoming a little disjointed—some of them must have been forced to start over from the beginning to restore the broken spots. The knights pressed on regardless, with no hesitation in their steps. They were already reaching full speed.

An instant before the forces clashed, the orcs unleashed their third volley point-blank. A bright blue light flashed over the entire formation; the next instant, the knights disappeared from view in a cloud of black smoke.

The roar of the guns reached my ears a moment later, then the sound of the horsemen smashing through the spears and the screams of beasts, both horse and orc. The priests' incantation was becoming more and more unsynchronized. The tremor of hooves rose once more, and finally, the foot soldiers disappeared into the smoke.

At length, a strong gust of wind cleared the fumes away and I could see again. By then, the last of the horses had almost disappeared beyond the hills, where foot soldiers were taking on the remaining orcs. While the hill orcs still outnumbered their enemies, they had completely lost the will to fight. In a one-sided pursuit, the human infantry simply chased and slaughtered them as they screamed and ran. In no time at all, the hill was red with blood.

A horn echoed from beyond the hills, signaling the discovery of more enemy forces and a continuation of the charge. Princess Liana's expression stiffened as she absorbed its message.

"Confirm the situation! Have the Templars advance to the hilltop! Hero, come with—"

Her face was turned halfway toward me when a thundering roar cut her off. Clearly different from the preceding gunshots, this sound had to mean that now they were firing cannons.

Liana's complexion paled visibly, the color draining from her lips.

"I told them so many times...!" she murmured.

We'd already known it was going to be a trap; that was why the plan was to turn back if the enemy was too numerous. However, it wasn't so simple to stop a group of horsemen after they initiated a charge. Once the riders' bloodlust was riled up, they couldn't be expected to make level-headed decisions—all the more when they were proud, prestigious warrior types. Their greatest fear was to be seen as cowards.

The next sound that rang out over the hills was a united chorus of guns, which was quickly followed by a second volley. The priests gave up on the barrier-maintaining chant as every defense was breached. With fatigue on their faces, their cohesion lost, each individually stumbled back into the chant required to re-erect the barriers from the ground up. Next came the roar of the third volley, and then, finally, the horrific sound of cavalry colliding with infantry.

The princess cried out "Hurry!" but we were already picking up the pace. I was the first to reach the hilltop, but there was too much smoke covering the battlefield below for me to make out the details. I could only tell from the cycle of guns and the horses' brays that the combat still raged on.

The princess and her knights arrived shortly after me, and we watched as the smoke thinned bit by bit. First, I saw the forms of knights felled by gunfire, then orc soldiers crushed flat by the horses, with a few trampled knights among them. Then I fully took in the disastrous scene. Stretched across the valley at the base of the hills was a legion of orcs in a checkerboard formation. The knights had managed to cleave through some of the squadrons with their fierce charge. Unfortunately, that put them smack-dab in the center of enemy lines, and they were nearly surrounded.

A number of gunners were stationed around the orc legion, and they would eagerly rain gunfire upon any knight who tried to approach. As orcs were so short, they had to crane their necks to see soldiers on horseback, so they were at no risk of catching their brethren in the crossfire. What's more, this caldera of gunfire sprouted countless sharp thorns as well as the orcs' long spears. If a rider on the perimeter fell from his horse, these spears would rain down on him.

Had the allied army's commander already fallen? Their forces seemed to spiral into chaos. Some men simply dawdled where they stood, while others recklessly sliced deeper and deeper into enemy formations. Others still, perhaps having lost their sense of direction in the smoke, wove through the gaps as they strayed into the enemy's midst on their own.

Each time the guns roared, more of them would fall to the ground. Over half had already sunk into pools of blood, and it was only a matter of time for the rest.

"Blow the retreat horn!"

Immediately on the princess's order, a shrill horn sounded. It was already too late. The orcs that the troops had smashed through to get there had already regrouped behind them and were on the verge of restoring their formations. Once those were complete, the riders would have nowhere to run.

"Start chanting!"

The princess's words made me doubt my ears, but the faithful Knights Templar began their chant without a complaint. They readied themselves to attack.

I could no longer stay silent. "Your Highness," I said. "It's already too late."

"I know. But even if only a handful can be saved, I must continue to fight."

"And in exchange, you'll lose your Knights Templar. That's not a fair trade."

"It will take over a decade to reconstruct the Knights Templar, yes. But if we abandon those men without shedding a single drop of our own blood, the royal family will lose all its credibility. That would mean losing the force unifying humanity. We would be dragged back to the days of fighting among ourselves, and should it come to that, we'll have lost over a hundred years of progress. That is why my blood must be shed, here and now."

She made her decision, staring far, far into the future. *I guess that's precisely why that young woman became the Princess Knight who tied the lords' armies together. Far more than those foolhardy daredevils deserved, if you ask me.*

Still, her decision was most likely the right one.

Then let me ride with you, is what I would have liked to say. But I still didn't have a grasp on how much power I would be able to wield here. *I only play the game once I know my own hand.*

"Hero, please return to camp. Tell Rigel to take the priest and withdraw."

After a moment, I said, "Godspeed."

"I pray your good fortune carries on as well, dear hero. Please save humanity in my place."

"I will, without fail."

"And my brother too."

My nod brought a relieved smile to her face. She turned back to the enemy, calling out another order.

"Charge!" she cried, a fearless smile on her face.

Knights clad in pure-white armor and wielding shields and spears of light raced down into a tempest of devastation, a whirlwind of iron and flames.

As I watched them go, I pondered: *How am I going to save this world?*

✦

It started off as a rather unremarkable day. My high school entrance exams were approaching, and I was thinking pointless escapist thoughts as I stretched out in my chair. *Won't someone blast me off to another world, where I can be a hero?* I thought. And that was exactly what happened.

One moment, I felt as if someone had answered in the affirmative. The next, I was plunged into water.

Luckily for me, the water was shallow, and as I sprang up, I came face-to-face with a naked young woman. She introduced herself as the water priestess and pleaded for me to save the world. I became a hero and, without any real grasp of the situation, spent my days fighting alongside her. After five years, I managed to defeat the demon lord, and thus the world was saved. It was a harsh but wonderful adventure.

Then, on the night I was supposed to be wed to the water priestess, I was returned to my original world. Thankfully, I was no Urashima Tarou returning to find that everyone I knew had died long ago. Only half a year had passed in my home world. All the wounds I had accumulated over five years had vanished, and my well-tempered body had turned back into the feeble one I had before being summoned. In addition, I missed my exam date by quite a while.

Over the next ten years, I would frequently be sent off to other worlds by an unknown entity of whom I could detect nothing but a presence. Each time, I would save the world.

This new world I'd found myself in was my thirteenth.

'|X|'

We proceeded north down the cobblestone highway. No— we were retreating, so it would be more accurate to say we were *receding* north. Both tired horses and tired men stared at the ground with weary expressions, dragging their feet. I couldn't blame them. Ever since the defeat of the previous day, they had been marching without rest or sleep.

The only thing that kept them going was fear of the enemy's pursuit. Humans captured by orcs were apparently flayed alive and had their flesh devoured right before their own eyes. Quite a bone-chilling thought.

The road had been abandoned for quite some time and the stones were worn, but it was still faster than riding through the plains. We'd covered some distance, but the enemy probably had as well. Luckily, the orcs had yet to catch up. A backward glance revealed at most the smoke of a burning water mill.

Sir Rigel was in a state of despair. Despite the fact that she had willingly sacrificed herself, he couldn't bear the thought that he failed to protect the princess, whom he had served since she was young.

"If we are to count our blessings, we're lucky that our army fell beyond the hill," Rigel muttered in a self-deprecating tone.

"Yes, I guess so."

What would have happened if that slaughter had taken place where our remaining forces could see it? I suspected the noncombatants would have scattered and fled from fear, to be shamefully captured not far from the battlefield.

Luckily, that wasn't how it went off. We managed to make an orderly shift to retreat. This was likely thanks to Rigel's level-headed command, and we were fortunate for it. After all, priests were, in a sense, more valuable than knights. Extracting them largely unscathed was a huge accomplishment, although we did end up abandoning a large portion of our food and supplies.

We also had the Knights Templar to thank for the enemy's delayed pursuit. The survivors of the allied forces reported that the Templars fought magnificently. Brandishing their spears of light as they stampeded through enemy lines, only five hundred riders in three columns, they pressed on and on in an attempt to take out the orc's strategic headquarters. Unfortunately, they were too greatly outnumbered and lost momentum with each corpse they trod over. Once they had lost two of their columns, they ran out of steam, their feeble remnants swallowed up by the enemy horde, flag and all.

The hundred surviving knights of the allied armies managed to make use of the confusion. With the help of the foot soldiers who had remained atop the hill to treat the injured, they managed to break away. Of course, that information only served to darken Rigel's spirits further. He had been protected by the death of the person he was supposed to protect.

What were her final moments like? I'd heard that a horrid fate awaited women captured by orcs, different from how they treated the men. I found myself praying that she met a warrior's end.

Now a warning rose behind us. I turned to see a pack of bizarre creatures leaping out of the forest we had just passed through. They were similar to wolves but boasted sharp, falcon-like beaks where their mouths should have been. And on their backs rode those irksome orcs. It looked like there were roughly a hundred of them. Their vanguard had finally caught up to us. I could see the forlorn survivors in our rear guard preparing to flee.

Perfect. This was just the chance I needed to test out my hero's powers. An excellent opportunity to see how effective they were against my foes in this world.

"Rigel, I'm going to fight."

"Be careful! They have short guns!"

I spurred my horse and activated my shield of light. This was the same magic the Knights Templar used. I had the ability to instinctively pick up the flow of mana and understand how to apply it, which allowed me to replicate nearly any of a world's spells after seeing them once. This was one of the graces bestowed upon me by the mysterious entity who sent me to this world.

At a full gallop, I leapt over the knights who were frantically forming a line opposite the orcs. A one-eyed orc at the front—presumably their leader—immediately fired on me. A metallic *ping* resonated as the bullet was deflected off the shield of light.

The orcs spread out around me, guns pointed. I deployed shields on both hands and waited for them to fire. The next instant, shots assailed me from all sides. A shrill shriek echoed in my ears and the shields glowed under the barrage with a light that dazzled my eyes.

I managed to endure it, and when they saw that I was unharmed, the orcs were clearly flustered. That was my chance. I dispelled the shield on my right hand, replacing it with a spear of light. Then I threw the spear at the orc closest to me, piercing its heart.

I quickly manifested another spear and searched out the orc with one eye. He had already turned his back and was retreating with the other orc riders who had used up their shots. Was he going to reload and reengage? *Not on my watch, he isn't.* I locked my aim and lobbed the spear. It left a trail of light in its wake as it flew at my foe.

But the instant before it made contact, the one-eyed orc wrenched his body to the side. The blade grazed his flank as it flew past and, although thrown off balance, he managed to cling to the saddle. Apparently, he could evade a surprise attack from behind on pure instinct. *What a monster!*

Before I could go after him again, orc riders flooded into the space between us from both flanks to shield him. I threw the spear that had already manifested in my hand at a different rider and manifested shields on both hands again. The spear grazed my target's cheek, and half the orcs fired upon me in unison.

Under twice as many hits this time, the shield finally reached its breaking point. I could feel the sensation of vast quantities of mana draining from my body. *So that was why the priests looked so depleted in battle. The greatest loss of mana is when the shield breaks.*

The remaining orcs maintained their position, their guns fixed on me, but clearly more wary of the possibility of an attack coming from behind me. *I see. I definitely do look like a decoy, judging by my actions. What splendid coordination.*

Looking back, I saw that my allies were still quite a ways away. It was time to call it quits and rejoin them. I lowered my speed and fell farther back from the orcs. In my irritation, I manifested a spear and hurled it at One-Eye as he raced to the front once more. The light weakened as the spear flew, dissipating entirely before it reached him.

The orcs disappeared into the forest. I halted my horse and waited for my allies to catch up. *I've driven the enemy off for the time being, but I didn't do any significant damage. They'll attack again soon.*

·|ɴ|·

I was welcomed back with jubilation.

"As expected of a hero! A wonderful sight to behold!"

"To think you could fight off so many alone!"

"You fight with the strength of many men."

The knights surrounded me and showered me with praise. By the look on his face, I'd exceeded even Rigel's expectations.

"I was watching. I didn't think you were that powerful! I see why God chose you!"

"No need to make such a fuss. I only took out one of them."

"Humility turns to cynicism at its extremes. Only a handful of the Knights Templar could use magic without any blessed equipment. Even *with* the equipment, I know of none who could withstand so many bullets with a shield. Additionally, it's unprecedented to see a spear of light thrown like that. They normally disappear the moment they've been cut off from their power source."

I see. As usual, my mana level is apparently far greater than what is normal here.

"I'm sure the Black Dog fled the moment he realized your strength. It was, admittedly, a modest victory. But you have allowed us to regain our hope."

I could understand why they'd celebrate a small victory after such an enormous loss, but I didn't have the slightest feeling that I'd won anything at all. On even the most generous interpretation, it was a draw.

"By the way, who's the Black Dog?" I asked.

"Ah, you haven't heard about him yet. He was the orc riding the black beak-dog."

The one-eyed one, then. And the beasts are called beak-dogs.

Rigel went on. "He is the craftiest and most resourceful of the orcish generals. He and his riders have plagued us for the past seven or eight years. He appears without warning, taking out smaller units. Many brave and virtuous knights have fallen to him."

A war hero of the orcs. A champion. No wonder he was so formidable. Wait, don't tell me...

"Let me guess. The orcs began using guns around the same time he appeared."

"No, the guns themselves have been around for a while now. But there weren't so many of them when I was a lad, and they could not break through magic. They were only useful for making loud noises to spook the horses. But, as you can see, they are now quite a threat."

My heart sank. That was even worse. The orcs had not been handed guns by some cheat-like entity. They had discovered and developed them themselves.

In all the worlds I'd saved thus far, humanity had been winning on its own merit. The world's predicament was triggered by a particular entity—a demon lord with fearsome powers, the sudden mutation of a monster, an ancient weapon with enough power to end all life as we knew it—that sort of thing. As long as I could do something about that one problem, I could save the world. That was my job.

But it looked like this world ran on different rules. Without relying on any special powers, the enemy was overwhelming humanity, solely with their own might. And it wasn't just numbers—they had the technological advantage as well.

There was a good chance we were losing to them as a civilization. I mean, they had managed to gather so many guns and soldiers on a single battlefield. This had gone beyond the point where I could do anything simply by being peerless. What's more, considering the fight I put up today, I highly doubted I could even call myself peerless.

In that case, why not use my knowledge to improve the human's weaponry in this world? Rejected. I'd tried that before, and the result had been a mess. Sure, a matchlock looks simple, but it is the culmination of the art of metallurgy and requires the understanding of many other technologies. Just knowing the basic structure didn't get me anywhere. It was fundamentally pointless unless the world had already developed the necessary basic skills. And bringing those fundamental techniques to another world would be even more difficult.

Remember, in the real world, I was little more than a useless bum who'd barely graduated junior high. I was never going to forget how a gun based on my vague recollections blew off the arm of a young blacksmith apprentice when he tried to test fire.

Ultimately, all I could do was use the powers given to me by some unknown being to swing a sword around. In most cases, it was far quicker to take the enemy's head than it was to reform political affairs. That had been enough to save every world so far. In fact, I'd saved twelve worlds that way. There was only one thing I was capable of: fight, fight, and fight to the death. Yes, to the death. I was confident I wouldn't lose to anyone.

I suddenly felt the proud and expectant presence of that unknown entity behind me. It seemed to say, *"Don't worry. You can do it."*

How irresponsible. Goddammit, don't egg me on.

A question crossed my mind. *What happens if I die in another world?* Strangely, this was rarely more than a passing thought. I always had the vague impression that I couldn't die. *It would be all right. I was the hero, after all.* It was scary, but in the same way that riding a roller coaster was scary.

So why was this world suddenly filling me with existential dread?

Oh well, thinking about it wasn't going to get me anywhere. I had no idea what would happen after I croaked in my own world either. It was no different here.

✴

After the skirmish, in the forest near Dragonjaw Gate, the orc whom the hairless monkeys called the Black Dog staggered as he dismounted his aquilup. Even with the help of his subordinates, he could barely stay upright. He had lost more blood than he had expected, and he grimaced at the dull pain that raced down his flank.

A perfect semicircle had been gouged out of his side, armor and all. It was pure luck that the attack had missed his organs. Had he not coincidentally turned to check on a subordinate toppling from his mount, that spear of light would have pierced straight through his heart. He had to admit that he had let his guard down. The major clash had dealt a vital blow to the enemy. He had been convinced they would no longer have any will to fight.

Something had definitely felt a little off. He should have noticed it sooner. How had they managed to retreat so quickly after such a massive loss? When that hairless monkey rushed to the front alone, he had simply appeared to be someone with a death wish. But what was the truth of the matter? Neither the Black Dog nor his men had ever come across a monkey who fought like that.

They had encountered men who wielded those glowing spears and shields before—they had taken down a number of them in just the last battle. But the one in white armor was so strong, there was no comparison. The monkey had repelled their volley. He threw the spear. He could switch between weapons in an instant. What else could he be but a monster?

However, a number of his men reported seeing the monkey's shield break from the last barrage. Perhaps they would have been able to take him out if the battle had continued. The Black Dog shook the thought out of his head.

Witnessing that battle had revived the enemy cavalry's fighting spirit. They were reconstructing their formation. If there was another clash, both sides would face significant casualties. While it might provide a chance for them to kill the powerful monkey, it was not worth sacrificing the lives of his comrades.

Aquilup riders were valuable, as aquilups only bonded with the first creature they saw after hatching from their eggs. What's more, they only produced eggs in the wild. The art of taking those rare eggs from the nest and then incubating, hatching, and raising them was a secret passed down only to the warriors of his tribe.

But more than that, he loved his subordinates.

Perhaps he would have made a different decision if he were uninjured. However, when he was badly wounded, unable to give level-headed orders, he couldn't possibly subject his men to an unknown threat. Or perhaps things would have been different if he had taken a battery of foot soldiers with him.

We'd have the foot soldiers if that margrave's no-good son hadn't opened his mouth. He cursed. But it was too late to do anything about the matter.

Before long, a recon party returned with the orc who had died in battle. The Black Dog recognized him as his sister's husband. He was a splendid young man, the best or second-best rider in the village. The couple got along well; they had been blessed with their first child right before he embarked on this campaign. His heart sank even further as he considered the letter he would need to write home.

The Black Dog made his resolution. He would settle this score if it was the last thing he did. No matter how preposterous that man was, he couldn't be immortal. Surely he could be taken out with proper preparations. *More importantly, I can tell that monkey will be the biggest obstacle—no, a stepping stone—to my ambitions.*

Whatever the case, he would kill that man in the next bout. Such ambitions were the reason he led his comrades into battle, were they not?

As we left the forest, the voices of the troops began to rise in celebration. Each and every one of them forgot their fatigue as they frolicked and rejoiced. Ahead of us, a massive mountain range towered, blocking our way like a wall. Even though it was still quite a distance away, I had to crane my neck to see its summit. It would not be feasible to cross these mountains on foot.

Of course, these cliffs were not the reason for the jubilation. Hands, waving gaily, pointed out the gate built into a narrow valley between the mountains. Commonly called Dragonjaw Gate, it was the sole passage through Dragonbone Ridge, the boundary between the worlds of orc and humanity. Our goal was finally in sight.

"Hear me, hear me! Keep your guard up! Those dogs are still hot on our scent!" Rigel tried to rein them in, but even he was unable to conceal the hint of relief in his voice.

As luck would have it, we managed to reach the gate without facing another attack. Dragonjaw Gate was more like a massive dam than a fortress. The Dragonbone Ridge was so huge by comparison that the gate's true size was impossible to grasp from afar. Up close, it overwhelmed the senses with its sheer height and bulk. Rigel told me that the walls were approximately 1.2 kilometers across, forty meters thick at the thickest point, and a towering two hundred meters high. While the walls looked like slabs of concrete, they were actually constructed from stone, but one would have to go right up to them and peer closely to see the joints between the piled-up stones.

Snowmelt from the mountains pooled on the other side of the gate's protective walls. If needed, the floodgates—carved with a massive water dragon, thus the name—could be opened, and the narrow pass would fill with enough water to wash away any encroaching army.

According to legend, back in the times when humanity ruled much of this world, a great magician employed giants to build this gate. While I couldn't know the truth of the matter, it would certainly be a trial and a half to construct such a thing without magic. Maybe, just maybe, the magician had been an otherworlder like me—although one with skills that I most definitely lacked.

The strongest fortification of Dragonjaw Gate actually lay beneath it: a massive magic circle laid by that same great magician. Using the mana flowing through the earth, it covered the entirety of the protective walls with a barrier that blocked any and all projectiles. As a matter of fact, I was summoned here on top of that very circle.

This gate was probably the reason this world's humans showed so little concern about the orcs. Protected by such a peerless fortress, they felt little danger. However, the fact that I had been summoned surely meant there was some crisis threatening humanity itself. Things were definitely not as peaceful as they seemed.

⋮⦚⋮

The head of Dragonjaw Gate's defensive garrison came out to greet us. His name was Herbert, as I recalled. Cordial and trusted by the guards, he was a living rags-to-riches story, a poor farmer who'd risen to success via his accomplishments in the military.

I'd met him when I was summoned, and I found him to be a cheerful, sociable old man. I was surprised to see that his expression now was stiff.

"You've returned early... Where might Her Highness be?" he asked timidly after letting us in.

Herbert had looked after the princess with Rigel when she was young and was still one of her most ardent devotees. When we set out, he'd pleaded with me to protect her. I remember him saying something like *"Her Highness has been blessed with a rare knack for strategy, but she can at times be oblivious to danger. A show of courage from the general may pep up the soldiers, but that mustn't be taken too far... Oh, Hero! Please, protect Her Highness! Surely that is why God sent us his chosen. Please help her."*

Rigel remained silent. The reduced forces that had staggered back, the wagons full of the injured, the ragged priests, and, more than anything, the look on his face should have made it obvious what had happened. Still, Herbert needed to hear it to be sure.

He spoke in as cheery a voice as he could muster. "I see it now. Her Highness sent the priests home so she could take command of the pursuit. You can't move fast with priests, after all! She'll be back soon, won't she? Shall I keep the door open for her? Once the gate is shut, it's quite troublesome to—"

"Her Highness isn't coming back." Rigel cut him off, his voice tight. "They'll catch up soon. Close the gate."

"Then the princess is..."

"I'm ashamed to say."

The two old men fell silent.

We stayed in Dragonjaw Gate for a full day to recover the strength we would need for the trek to the capital. Three days of marching without rest was harsh on the priests and attendants, and the soldiers and dragon riders needed the rest as well.

A room with a roof, and warm meals. Pretty simple, yet it felt like the finest luxury.

I awoke the next morning to the sound of garrison soldiers racing around the barracks. I arbitrarily nabbed someone and asked what was going on, only to find out the orcs had appeared at the entrance to the valley. An emergency order had been issued. I gave the soldier my thanks, got my appearance in order, and made for the watch tower where the head of the garrison was supposed to be.

Sir Rigel was one step ahead of me, deep in discussion as he and Herbert glared out at the orcs. Noticing I'd arrived, they bowed to me briefly and then turned back to the enemy again. Herbert's eyes were so sharp, I could hardly recognize him as the same despondent old man I'd seen only yesterday.

"I never thought I'd see the day when orcs would advance on these walls," Herbert said with a groan.

"I don't know what to say."

"I'm not chastising you, Rigel. But with those numbers... I didn't doubt your report, but I didn't truly believe it until I saw it for myself."

The orcish legions were gushing forth from the forest near the mouth of the valley. Their front line was already in formation at the entrance, and there they seemed to come to a halt.

"Are they blocking off the pass? If they came up to us, we'd flood them out," Herbert said.

"That will make it difficult for our other expeditions to return."

"Hmph, a fitting end for those impudent fools who ignored Her Majesty's summons and went off to line their own pockets."

"But that will leave this year's harvest at a terrible low. Her Majesty would not have wanted the people to starve." Rigel spoke calmly. Still... What were they talking about? I thought I got the general idea but needed to be sure.

"Sir Rigel, there were expeditions besides ours? Also, what is this harvest you speak of?"

"You weren't informed? Then let me explain."

"If you would."

"To start with, the orcs are a foul race that was created by the False God when the world was first formed. Therefore, it stands to reason that vanquishing them is the duty of every knight. For fame and virtue, the feudal lords have each formed subjugation forces in their own territories."

"I see. Then the other expeditions would be those detached units."

"Indeed. Once upon a time, the orcs resided in the distant wasteland of the south. However, in the past hundred years they've migrated north. Now they've built settlements only a few days from the mountains. We must push their territory south again. As I said, it's a knight's duty to subjugate them."

"And what about the harvest?"

"Truth be told, fame and virtue aren't enough to move anyone. Even amassing an army takes money."

"That's the feudal lords' main objective," Herbert cut in. "Alongside defeating orcs, they also take the food and goods they find at their settlements. It's an outrageously profitable enterprise. That's how I made a name for myself."

Pretty much what I expected.

Rigel went on, "As you might imagine, the orcs don't always submit. They will, at times, gather numbers and resist. In those cases, it is the duty of the monarchy to unite our forces and fight them off. On this campaign, when we heard the orcs had amassed a great army in response to our invasion, we sent a summons to the subjugation parties that were already on that side of the gate." He sighed. "But only half of them gathered. Worse yet, our dragons chose that time to go to the peaks."

It seemed that I had been summoned as this unit was coming together. Meaning that the folks of this world called me with the intention of having me aid their pillaging. *Hey, I've been summoned for stupid reasons before. If I'm remembering right, I ended up in my fourth world when someone tried to summon a "helper demon" to find a lost item.*

The intent of the summoner notwithstanding, whenever I'd been summoned, there was always some crisis putting the world at risk. Whether I fulfilled the goal of the summoner or not, I couldn't return until the world was saved. *Right, I never did end up finding what they lost.*

I just wanted to finish things quickly and go home. This would be my thirteenth disappearance. My mother probably wouldn't be too worried at this point, but some...troublesome things might happen if I took too long. Who's to say my mother wouldn't finally give up on me while I was gone and leave my room an empty shell? *If that room goes away, I'll have nowhere left to go. That would be troublesome indeed.*

Now, back on topic.

"You're saying that the subjugation forces that didn't answer Her Highness's summons are stranded on the other side of that orc army."

"That they are. But they get what they deserve. Had they marched with Her Highness, perhaps the war would have turned out differently," Herbert said with disgust.

But I had to wonder. Even if we'd had double the troops, I doubted we would have been able to win in those circumstances.

Small firearms echoed at the mouth of the valley. I focused my eyes but couldn't see where they had been fired from. Most likely a blind spot from here. Would those stranded armies try to return, oblivious, only to run into the orcish legions? Perhaps they would try to force their way through.

"There's nothing we can do," Rigel said. "Time is of the essence. We must return to the capital and report the gravity of the situation."

With Rigel urging me on, I turned to the stairs. I needed to get ready to go.

Our arrival at Dragonjaw Gate marked the dissolution of the allied armies, who had united for the sole purpose of combating the orcs. The few survivors were offered meager travel fees and food—little reward for their efforts and losses. But they took it with lips shut and set off to their homelands. Modest as the rewards were, they were lucky that they even had their wounds treated. The title-less mercenaries were not provided even that.

Taking along a few of the major priests, Rigel and I hurried down the road to the capital.

CHAPTER 2
TO BE HIS MAJESTY'S SWORD

THE PATH TO THE CAPITAL was uncannily peaceful.

We passed through a number of villages and were welcomed by none of them. The villagers shut their doors and timidly peeked at us through the cracks. Yet it didn't quite seem that they feared our army—rather that the rumors of our defeat had arrived faster than we had.

It was a rather boring journey, so I asked Rigel about what had been on my mind.

"Is it possible to make peace with the orcs?"

He looked at me as if I had turned into some incomprehensible oddity. After a pause, he replied wearily, "Oh, a joke. Your otherworld humor is too much for an old man to handle."

"I'm being serious."

The look in his eyes changed to one of genuine concern. "Hero, we're only a short hop from the capital. You will be able to rest as much as you want once we arrive. Please keep your wits about you."

"I'm not tired."

Now misgivings began to show in his expression. He peered curiously into my eyes, weighing their sincerity. *No, it's most likely my sanity he's judging instead. Evidently, it's considerably odd to even consider the possibility of peace in this world.*

"Hero, they are vile life-forms spawned from the False God. Peace is a dream within a dream. I highly doubt they even have the intellect for it."

"You're the one who warned me not to make light of their intelligence. And from what I've seen in battle, at least, they seem to be quite smart. Perhaps negotiations are possible."

"You've only seen them in battle. When a pack of wolves venture out to hunt, they may appear to display coordination and unity, but that is not enough to deem them intelligent. Do you find merit in negotiating with beasts?"

Hey now, you know those orcs did more than that. I opened my mouth to argue, but before I could speak, Rigel went on.

"Of course, it's foolish to underestimate their abilities. But those extend no further than the battlefield. It is a complete mistake to take them as humanity's equal simply because they are strong in battle. Why, the mere thought of permitting the existence of those filthy, vile beings repulses me. To destroy them is God's will. It is the duty of every knight!"

His expression was serious. I had thought that he evaluated the orcs more levelheadedly than the others, but by his own words, that *extended no further than the battlefield.* Under the circumstances, there was no point in continuing the conversation.

"I see. You may have a point," I said, bringing an end to the discussion.

The next few moments were occupied by an awkward silence. Then Rigel looked around warily, his eyes coming to rest on the priests a short distance away. He made sure they weren't paying attention before bringing his bearded mouth to my ear.

"I cannot bring myself to endorse your ideas. But still, I must offer you a word of advice."

"What is it?"

"Be mindful of who you share such words with. Especially around the priests. It's possible even the hero may be deemed a heretic."

While his eyes were stern, they were also the eyes of a kind old knight. He still worried for me despite our disagreement. And for my part, despite those differences, I was taking to him even more.

†|x|†

The palace was on a hill right below Dragon Peak, the highest and most conspicuous point of Dragonbone Ridge. Its accompanying city spread out from the base of the hill, surrounded by walls built of white stone. It was large, magnificent, and beautiful, but all in all a bit underwhelming after I'd just seen Dragonjaw Gate. It was probably unreasonable of me to compare this human construction to a relic of ancient magic.

The first three days after my arrival were wasted learning etiquette. They wanted me to take part in the reporting ceremony, where we'd inform the king of our results. It was just a report, but it was made into a big deal because it was an official royal duty.

It's the same in any world, really.

Even though I only had to know the manners pertaining to the reporting ceremony, there was much to learn. I was taught the timeline of the event, how to enter the grand hall, what posture to wait in until I was called, how to respond to the minister of ceremonies, and so on. So many things were determined down to the minutest details. The royal court even dispatched an etiquette tutor specifically to teach me. Naturally, teaching took more than kindness. My tutor was a large and muscular man whose cheek had been marked by a sword.

"A hero must conduct himself as a perfect hero. That is what His Majesty demands." That was the very first thing he told me. Evidently, my role in the country had already been decided.

It was a bother, but I had little to lose by playing my part. That was an important lesson I'd hammered into myself from my first few worlds. There was a time where my poor manners made the nobles take me for a fool and refuse to cooperate. At other times, I had enraged them and nearly lost my life for it.

The day of the ceremony came. Rigel prepared my clothes for me, and after I'd finished changing into them, he looked me over with fondness in his eyes, like the sight of me had stirred up old memories. The unkempt beard that he worked so hard to shove under his helmet on the battlefield was now done up in two tidy bundles.

"That's the formal wear of the dragon riders. You wear it well. Yes, I can confidently send you out before His Majesty like that."

"Thank you." I took a better look at myself. The deep gray looked plain at first glance, but on closer inspection, I saw subtle ornamentation on the high-quality cloth. The tailoring was perfect and clearly expensive. I had to wonder where the clothes came from. They didn't seem like they had been hurriedly made for me. While it was faint, I had the sense that someone else's arms had passed through these sleeves before. Not an old man like Rigel, that I was sure of. He was quite a bit smaller than me, in any case.

A boy wearing the same formal uniform entered the room. Something about him reminded me of Rigel. He looked at me dubiously upon seeing what I was wearing.

"What's wrong, Kyel?" Rigel asked him.

"I came to inform you that we are ready to depart."

"Understood. We've just finished up here too. We'll be out at once." Rigel turned back to me. "Well then, Hero. Shall we get going?"

The path to the palace was jam-packed with people. The dragon riders guiding us were forced to raise their voices and part the crowds with their horses.

"Quite a lively town."

"The road from the west gate to the temple is the busiest one. These parts are usually supposed to be quieter."

"Did something happen?"

"Well... Word on the street is that our savior has appeared."

Meaning they came to see me.

"Word spreads fast."

"That it does. I'm sure everyone's just starved for good news... I'm counting on it to drown out the pain of our loss."

I see, so that's your game.

"So then... Should I wave?"

"Just carry yourself boldly. That should do the trick."

We purposely took the long way around before coming out onto the main road. Our horses pressed on toward the palace under the watchful eyes of many onlookers.

'|✕|'

The palace stood on a jagged hill dotted with exposed stone, the Dragon Peak towering over it. A wide moat and a sturdy wall on the outer shore blocked out any foreign intruders. The road from the city to the palace came to a halt at a stone bridge, where our way was blocked by the castle gate. There was a massive tower on each side with cross-shaped crenels forming orderly patterns around the walls. Their looming aura would surely intimidate anyone who tried to pass.

When I looked farther up the hill, I could see yet another layer of walls and a winding path stretching from gate to gate. The castle stood tall at the summit of the hill, shaped like a box with a domed roof. At each of its four corners stood a dignified, unornamented tower. It was made from the same white stone as the city walls, but with the steep bare rock of the ridge as its backdrop, it gave off an impression more cold than elegant. From the very center of the dome, a watchtower protruded like a spear thrust at the heavens. It could be seen from almost anywhere in town. To be blunt, it was more a fortress than it was a palace.

Once we were through the first gates, we dismounted our horses and left them at the stable. We parted ways with the attendants, guards, and other dragon knights for the time being, making for the palace under the direction of its sentinels.

On our way up the hill, a young knight caught up to us. He must have climbed in quite a hurry, as he was quite out of breath. He had my sympathy.

"My apologies! The streets were so crowded..."

I knew him already. His name was Thret, and he was one of the few knights who survived the engagement. He'd been chosen to give the report, as he was the survivor who came from the highest-ranked house. While his mind sometimes wandered, he had survived for a reason. Despite his youth, he had nerves of steel and could think on his feet. He would likely go far.

At the summit, a sentinel interrogated us. His questions were answered, loudly and theatrically, by the sentinel who had led us there.

"Dragon rider Captain Rigel and two others! They have come to report the results of the battle to His Majesty! I leave them in your hands!"

"Such is my duty! I shall show them the way!"

The door rose slowly, accompanied by rumbling and the clanking of heavy metal. We were led into a chamber the size of a tennis court. On the back wall was a conspicuously ornate door, and we were urged to form a single-file line in front of it.

"His Majesty awaits you ahead. Please wait until you are called."

The first sentinel left and was quickly replaced by two more wearing bright-red surcoats and glimmering chainmail without a speck of rust. Their hands were wrapped around spears ornamented with gold inlay. Once they took their positions, the sentinels turned to the door in perfect unison, then hit their spears against the ground twice. At that signal, the door opened with a loud creak.

The room that was revealed was as large as a gymnasium, with a ceiling that was twice as high as the one we were standing in. The walls were draped with banners boasting all manner of crests. I recognized a few as the ones the allied lords carried. Perhaps these were the crests of the lords who swore their allegiance to the king.

Light streamed in from the crenels that lined a platform around halfway up the walls. This platform was supported by a line of pillars that circled the room. A red carpet stretched from the entrance all the way to the back, and a great many people were crowded along both sides of it. About half were men and half women, and judging by their clothes, all were quite well bred. Their outfits seemed to grow more extravagant as I looked farther down the line. At the very back was a group dressed in white robes embroidered with gold and adorned with glimmering gemstones. *They must be the high priests,* I thought.

At the end of the carpet, on a throne one step higher than the rest of the room, sat a small figure. *So that's what the king looks like.* I'd been following Princess Liana ever since I was summoned at Dragonjaw Gate, so this was my first time meeting him.

"The dragon captain! The hero from another world! A knight whose life was saved by the princess! These three have come to seek your audience!"

When the sentinels inside the door announced our arrival, all eyes gathered on us—no, on me. I couldn't blame anyone for staring at a man who had appeared with such a dubious title. I'd grown used to being looked at with such eyes.

We matched pace with the sentinels, proceeding out before the king, kneeling, keeping our heads down. Waiting.

"Raise your heads."

I looked up at the surprisingly high-pitched voice.

Sitting on the throne with his chest puffed out was a young boy. His pretty face was spoiled by a grimace that didn't suit him at all. He was clearly trying to exude as much dignity as he could muster, but to be honest, it wasn't going well. By arching his body to make it seem bigger, he only showed off how slender and weak it was. Even worse, his grim attitude only served to emphasize his failure to make an impression. Despite the fact that it was all somewhat comical, his obvious desperation made me feel sorry for him, and I hadn't the slightest urge to laugh.

I'd heard the boy was Princess Liana's younger brother. Some of his features were similar to hers, but the air he gave off was the polar opposite. Liana could draw people to her with her innate diligence and energy. The boy possessed neither.

What he wore instead was a heavy gloom—quite understandable given the position he had been forced to assume. As the king uniting humanity, the fate of his race rested on his shoulders.

We were losing the war, and he had just lost a blood relative. The situation was far too grave for a child to bear. And yet, the boy rose to the challenge, earnestly playing the part of a dignified king.

An urge to help him however I could began to grow within me. Luckily, I was the hero. Even if the role had been shoved onto me by an unknown someone, it was my mission to save the world. I would probably be of some use. The thought got me a little motivated.

After all the ceremonial exchanges, it was finally time for the report. First up was Rigel.

Rigel explained in detail what had led up to the engagement: How the dragon riders' scouting confirmed a mass gathering of orcs. How a royal decree was immediately issued to convene the lords who were out "subjugating" orcs. How, partway through the delivery process, the dragons went into breeding season, so the orders reached less than half of the lords—although here he had mixed in a lie, as over ninety percent of the messages had been delivered by that time. How, as they waited for the troops to gather, one of their priests received a divine revelation, held a summoning ceremony, and produced me. And finally, how the army marched to the field.

Beyond that, reporting what happened when we met the orcish armies was my duty.

An orcish legion of such magnitude, we could not see the horizon.
A shrill horn.
The heroic pounding of hooves.
Our knights pulverized their vanguard in one fell swoop.

The battle shifted to the area beyond the hill. Our knights built an army of orc corpses as they crossed the hill, only to find a vile, underhanded trap awaiting them. But those valiant men did not cower at the enemy's devices. They pressed on to break down the trap and took many of the foes down, but their numbers were too great. As the knights dug deeper and deeper into the enemy formation, they fell one by one to the orcs' cheap shots...

I didn't lie, per se. They did fight valiantly. They were just...a bit *too* valiant. When I told the story of the princess's charge, sobs began to fill the room. Whether this was acting or the effect of Liana's character, I couldn't say.

The report was *somewhat* exaggerated. We had decided on all the details beforehand. Rigel had already delivered the proper report on the day we arrived. This ceremony was more of an official presentation. Many of the people attending were relatives of the knights who died, and it would come back to bite me if I made them look bad.

In any case, that was all for my report. I took a step back and got down on one knee beside Rigel.

Thret spoke next, relating the tale of how he barely escaped the battlefield with his life. As he told it, he turned to flee the moment he heard the horn of retreat, but he was already surrounded by enemies. Many of his allies had fallen, and the rest had no way to escape. But then, at the instant he made peace with death, Liana's Knights Templar cut in like a white hurricane. The surviving combatants then rushed through the opening the knights created as fast as their horses could take them.

When he reached the top of the hill, he looked back to see the Knights Templar still endeavoring to aid the retreat. He saw the princess's flag fall. As much as he wanted to help, it was clear there was nothing he could do. And so, heartbroken, he left the battlefield to make sure that, at the very least, the lives she saved did not go to waste.

The suffering continued even after the battle was over. After marching day and night, there was an attack led by the Black Dog. They had only a hundred riders left against the Black Dog's force of five hundred beak-dogs, bolstered by countless foot soldiers and—*Hey, wait. Aren't you exaggerating a bit? This isn't what we discussed.*

I glanced at Rigel and saw that he had the same doubtful look on his face. *What was that man trying to do?*

Thret continued, claiming that the difference in numbers made him once again resolve to accept death. But there, light poured down from the heavens; the angels blew their horns. The hero's body began to glimmer in holy energy! With the power of God on his side, the hero rushed at the enemy, impaling the Black Dog with spear upon holy spear. The orc guns were rendered completely helpless, and the enemy fled in terror.

What monster was he talking about? That definitely wasn't me. I checked the faces of the gathered nobles. Some of their eyes were filled with awe. *You seriously believe that?*

But this was a lie that could be disproven all too easily. What's more, I'd be the one who got in trouble once the cat was out of the bag. Was he trying to harass me? No matter how I dug around in my memory, I couldn't think of anything I might have done to incur his wrath.

His report finished, Thret stepped back and kneeled beside me. He glanced at me with a grin. He didn't seem to mean any harm, but that just made his motives all the more incomprehensible. I would have to interrogate him later.

Next, the plan was to have the king praise me, to have him enlist my services as a knight sent by God, and to grant me a modest amount of territory—nonhereditary, though.

"Hero! I commend your bravery in challenging the enemy alone and assisting the retreat!" The young king followed the script with as much dignity as he could muster.

"Yes, sire! It is an honor to receive such praise!" I repeated my lines.

There, the king stopped for a moment. After a brief silence, he went off script. "Did my sister say anything at the end?"

"Yes, as I previously stated, she entrusted the stability of mankind to His Majesty, down to her last breath."

"That can't be everything. Did my sister say anything else?"

I couldn't discern his intentions. For the time being, an honest answer was probably best.

"She told me to save humanity. And to help His Majesty as well."

The king made a show of contemplating my answer. He had already received a detailed report from Rigel, so he shouldn't have needed to ask that question. This wasn't going according to plan.

The king addressed his priests. "Warsong Minister. Are we certain this man was sent by God?"

The face of the man who stepped up was familiar—it was the first face I saw upon coming to this world. This man had been responsible for coordinating the actions of the priests during the battle.

"Yes! I swear it in God's name. We carried out the ceremony as directed by divine revelation and witnessed him manifest from nothingness in a burst of light. There is no doubt he is the hero sent by God."

"I see. Does anyone have any doubts?"

The king took a sweeping glance over the nobles, making sure there were no objections.

"Then I must reward the man of God who drove back the enemy alone. I shall do so to the best of my abilities," he proclaimed. He seemed to think a bit more, then said, "To repay him with the same earthly titles we possess would be an affront to God. The reason for this being that God has already bestowed upon him the highest title of all."

Did he feel that the title of knight would be insufficient for the mascot he needed me to be? But he ran the risk of causing offense if he gave me too high a rank. *Ah, is that why he's contriving to work around the title?*

"Indeed, I see fit to reward him with prestigious land and status. I appoint the hero as the protector of Kadann Hill—the two villages at the base and the Hill Temple!"

Was that "something hill" the name of my territory?

Protector was the official title of the feudal lords in this world. Those appointed as protectors had the right to extract tax, labor, and occasionally military service from the villages in their territory. Two villages would provide more than enough revenue to ensure my standard of living.

Now some peculiar ruckus was beginning to break out. *Is the proposal really so strange? What is going on?*

"Your Majesty! Please reconsider!" a man cried out. He was well built, even bear-like, with bristle around his mouth. "You entrusted Kadann Hill to me just the other day! How could you give it to someone of such dubious origins?"

A priest in a conspicuously more extravagant robe snapped at him. "Silence! We have all recognized him as God's champion! Do you doubt the words of the church?!" *That priest was standing closest to the king, so he was probably at the top of the food chain.*

"N-no, not by any means. But still..."

"Then what basis have you to posit you are more worthy of that status than a messenger of God?"

That was all it took—the bear-man backed down.

"I-I simply strive to be useful to His Majesty..."

"Then follow his judgment."

"My apologies, Your Majesty. I have been impudent," the bear-man conceded. He withdrew meekly, but those eyes full of doubt still glared at me. *Quite a bothersome glare. Especially when I myself don't have the slightest clue what just happened.*

Judging by his clothing and his location in that grand hall, the bear-like man had to have been quite a high-ranking noble. I couldn't imagine why he would make such a fuss over a territory of just two villages. The surrounding clamor made me suspect that there was more to it.

Unfortunately, I didn't get a chance to ask. When the reporting ceremony ended, I left the same way I came, matching pace with two sentinels. The door to the grand hall closed behind us with a creak.

"Phew," I sighed. Then turned to Thret and asked, "What were you trying to do? That wasn't what we discussed."

"His Majesty demanded it. A messenger arrived just this morning and instructed me to glorify the hero's achievements. I actually held back, just so you know. They told me to report that you gave chase and slaughtered every last one of the enemies."

"We wouldn't have lost if we'd had a monster like that on our side. Why did we need to tell such a huge lie?"

"I mean, it's Kadann Hill after all. You'll need considerable accomplishments to claim it."

So it came back to that. *Is it that valuable?*

"Is the land fertile?"

"The land is under the king's direct control, and he has managed it well. I believe you can expect decent tax yields. Not that the land's particularly plentiful."

"Then why the fuss?"

"Kadann Hill is the holy land where generations of kings have been crowned," Sir Rigel cut in.

Ah, it's a holy land. No wonder it is such a prestigious place to hold.

Rigel continued, "Kadann Hill is under royal supervision, but whenever a field marshal is appointed, it's traditional to have them serve for a time as its protector."

"Field marshal?" The field marshals I knew of were the highest rank in the military, but that didn't seem to be the same in this world.

"The king's proxy, who controls the army in his place."

Hmm, I see. Then I was given the field marshal's land?

"Meaning, Hero, that you can now order military service from any lord who has sworn loyalty to the king."

I was speechless. This was a complete bolt from the blue. How was I supposed to react when such an enormous responsibility was thrust at me unasked? I said nothing in response as we walked on.

After descending the hill and reclaiming our horses from the stables, we were preparing to leave when a man arrived claiming to be a messenger from the king.

"His Majesty wishes to exchange some friendly words with the hero. You have been invited to join him for lunch. Please return to the palace."

He spoke directly to me. Apparently, I was the only one invited.

I turned, looking up at the impregnable fortress beyond the steep slopes. While I appreciated the offer, it would have been nice if he'd asked before I came all the way back down the hill. *Even with a hero's enhanced body, drudgery is still drudgery.*

"We have a lift for supplies over there," the messenger offered, reading my expression. "If you're tired, please feel free to use it."

What an excellent idea. If they have something like that, it would have been nice to use it the first time. I nodded and followed his directions.

The lift was installed in the steep cliff at the back of the palace. A large wooden pulley structure jutted out haphazardly from a stone warehouse overhead. Four thick chains dangled from it, fastened to large boards big enough to fit entire carriages.

"This is the lift," said the messenger. I took another look up the cliff. I was reminded of the time when I'd gazed up at the platform of Kiyomizu Temple in Kyoto. It was probably just as high.

Each time a strong wind blew, the air would pass through the chain links with a whistling scream. The board that was presented to me gave off a dull yet jarring sound. *Perhaps it would be better to walk up after all... His Majesty wanted a hero who acted like a hero, but how far am I supposed to go?*

"Please be at ease. The chains carry fully loaded wagons every day. The weight of one person isn't going to break anything." The messenger urged me to get on—alone. "Someone else will take over once you reach the top. Please follow his directions."

That was quite well prepared of him, to have someone stationed in advance. Yet despite how he talked up the safety of this thing, he clearly had no intention to ride it. Once he'd made sure I was firmly attached to the board with rope—*just in case*—he rang a bell attached to the system. After a moment, a similar bell answered above. I could hear the winding of rattling chains, and the board creaked and grated as it made its slow ascent. I assumed the irregular rhythm of the climb meant it was powered by human labor. *Perhaps I shouldn't be doing this.*

Each time the wind blew, the board swayed and the noises grew even worse. It was impossible to keep my balance without holding on to something. One unstable chain attached at a corner was the only thing supporting my body. I was, of course, tied to the opposite corner to balance it out. This left me in the perfect position to stare at the ground below. The messenger watched me for a while, but he saluted and left when I was about halfway up.

The terminus was a food storage depot, as I'd expected. I climbed the stairs in the back under the direction of a page who'd been waiting for me. Above the storage area was the kitchen, where cooks and servers shouted angrily as they moved in haste around the heat of the cauldrons. I carefully slipped through, trying not to get in the way, and found myself in a dim corridor.

The doors on the opposite side of the passageway all connected to that same hall the reporting ceremony was held in. Each time a server opened the door to pass through it, a rush of vibrant voices would burst out. According to the page, the nobles gathered in the room were being served a meal.

The stairs farther down the hall led us two floors up. The page told me that this was the floor for the king and his family. While there were a number of rooms, only one of them had guards. Coming to a stop in front of it, the page declared, "Your Majesty! I have brought the hero!"

The door swung open without a sound. This room was brighter than any of the others, mostly because of the large windows. There was a fireplace on the left-hand side, where the boy king sat with two sentinels standing by his side. Farther back, I saw an old man.

"You did well to come here. Please, take a seat."

The king offered me a seat by the fire. He still chose his words like a king, but his tone had softened quite a bit since I last saw him. I got the impression this was closer to his true self.

Once I was seated, the boy mischievously asked, "Now then, how did it feel to ride the lift?"

I thought about saying *Very entertaining*! to maintain the hero's dignity, but to tell the truth, I didn't want to be taken seriously and sent to ride it again.

"I have fought in many worlds as a hero, yet it was one of the most terrifying things I have experienced. I hope I'll never have to do it again," I answered honestly.

He seemed to take a liking to that response. "Ha ha ha! So it's terrifying even for a hero." Then his expression took a lonesome turn. "I'm sorry for that. You may be the hero, but there are those who would make a bit of a fuss if I invited you to my personal quarters. I wanted to avoid the public eye."

So that's why I was sent through the service door. The messenger did a good job steering me in that direction. Hats off to him.

"Thank you for your consideration. So then, how may I be of service?"

I was sure he had brought me here to discuss the offer to make me field marshal. In which case, I intended to turn it down. I hadn't been in this world very long, and I was still too ignorant of how it worked. How was I supposed to bring people together as would be expected of someone of that rank? But more to the point, I simply did not have the qualities of a leader. I'd picked up some interpersonal skills in various worlds but at my core, I was still an unsociable bum.

But instead, the king said, "I want to ask about my sister."

"I've already reported what I know."

"Not like that. You are the last person she spoke to. I want to hear her story and remember her. And perhaps a hero could see a side to her I could not."

Oh, so that's what he meant. I felt ashamed that I'd been readying myself for a political challenge. The ruler before my eyes, while a king, was only a young boy who had just lost his last living relative. I could understand him wanting to scrape together as many details as he could to bask in her memory.

When the food was brought in, His Majesty personally sliced the meat and set it on my plate. I nibbled on it as I told him everything I could remember about the princess.

"You sparred with her?"

"Yes, she challenged me the day after I was summoned."

"Who won?"

"I did, of course."

After a few exchanges, the princess had shouted at me to get serious. I decided it would be rude to continue holding back after she caught me at it, so I settled the match in the next strike.

The king's eyes opened wide. "You beat my sister?! That's quite an accomplishment."

"I learned my blade from the Sword Saint Owain," I said with pride.

"Who's that?"

"He was my master in the first world I saved."

I would always drop his name whenever my sword arm was praised. *Spreading his name to other worlds is the best memorial service I could give to that showoff. May his soul rest in peace.*

"I see. But I'm sure my sister was persistent."

"Yes, she kept challenging me until the sun set."

"Ha ha ha, she always was a sore loser."

I found it far easier to talk than I'd been expecting. I hadn't known the princess long, but strangely, I found a plethora of things to talk about. That was simply how fascinating she was. Again, I lamented her loss.

The stories went on and on until, finally, we came to that battle. The king stopped me there.

"That's enough. I know what happens next."

His voice was calm but anguished. He hung his head for a short while after that and then finally turned to the guards.

"I want to speak to him alone."

The guards disappeared without a word. Only the king, the old man, and I remained.

He was a peculiar old man, with a hook nose, a bald head, and very sharp eyes. He wore expensive clothes befitting an aide to the king, but they didn't suit him in the slightest. He simply stood there behind the king, totally lacking in presence, doing nothing, and ignored the order for everyone else to leave.

Who is he? Is he one of those things only I could see?

The king noticed my gaze. "You need not worry about him. He's loyal, despite how he looks."

On the king's word, the old man bowed ever so slightly. I gave him a nod back. He was apparently human.

Now the king spoke again. "It was I who killed my sister."

"What do you mean by that?"

"I've always been a sickly child. If I rode a horse for half a day, I'd be bedridden the next. And then, you know how my sister is. I can't remember how many times I heard the backbiting whispers of people wishing she were a man. Due to my condition, I could not lead the military, and my sister took up the role instead. If only I had been born stronger..."

The king cut himself off. It wasn't his fault he was born feeble. There was no reason for him to blame himself. But telling him that would provide no consolation. I couldn't find the right words.

"I always knew this day would come."

"She entrusted humanity's future to you in her last breath. She went out splendidly."

"I'm grateful that you think so. But to be honest, I'd have preferred for her to come home alive. Now there's no one left for me to rely on."

The king hung his head, and his slender shoulders quivered. I stood and placed a hand on his shoulder. I simply had to say it.

"That's not true, Your Majesty. You have me on your side. Just give the order."

He lifted his face, and his faintly reddened eyes took me in. "Really? Why would you go that far?"

"I swore it to the late princess. An oath to the dead is sacred, no matter the world."

"I see. Then I'll be counting on you."

A slight smile crossed his face. *Thank God.*

"Getting right to business, then, I'd like you to take up the role of field marshal."

I choked.

"What's wrong, Hero?"

"Y-yes, well, that was pretty sudden..."

"Has Rigel told you what sort of place Kadann Hill is?"

"He has."

"Then it should come as no surprise. Will you do it?"

"For His Highness's sake, I would cut down any enemy this sword can reach. But I'm not suited to be a general."

"Why is that?"

"I doubt the high nobles would follow the commands of someone like me. I believe such an important position should be entrusted to someone with a better understanding of this world."

"Someone like Galil?"

Galil? Who? That bear-man?

"He has a sense of duty," said the king. "He won't betray any-one. The more you believe in him, the more you depend on him, the more he will answer to your expectations. But that also means his hands are tied by so many obligations."

"Then what about Sir Rigel?"

"Old Rigel is even worse. He is incompetent when it comes to politics. He makes enemies unknowingly." The king took a deep breath. "Many houses lost their leaders in the last war. The situation is exceedingly unstable. For the time being, I cannot give anyone tied down by obligation—anyone of this world—the position of field marshal. Such fetters would one day spur them to turn on the rest of humanity, I'm sure of it. That said, I can-not leave the position empty either. If I leave it vacant, there's no telling who would try to worm their way into the gap. It can just be until I grow up—no, until the situation stabilizes somewhat! Please hear my wish!"

He looked desperate. My mind played back the last words I heard from Liana. "And my brother too." Having heard them, it was impossible to turn him down.

"I humbly accept."

"Great!" His Majesty's face lit up.

Thus, I became the field marshal.

After my meeting with the king was over, I left the palace incognito. Rather than the dragon rider uniform, I was clad in the same chainmail worn by the sentinels, and my face was completely covered by a bucket-like helmet. Officially, the hero had returned in the same carriage as Rigel.

Before I knew it, I had agreed to the position I'd intended to turn down. I'd always been a bit of a pushover, but this time, I'd completely caved with no resistance at all. But what could I do? Who could say no when that diligent young boy pleaded with such desperation in his eyes? *So be it. I've always been swept up by chance. It'll work out one way or another.*

Still, who had decided to install me as field marshal? I was concerned that it had been suddenly decided without any of the proper groundwork being laid. That old man was most suspicious. One look at his eyes was enough to know he wasn't just your average Joe. Perhaps he had curried favor with a young boy who'd lost his parents and was now controlling him from behind the scenes. The king seemed to trust him, calling him loyal. I would have to get a better understanding of the sort of individual he was. Perhaps Rigel knew something about him.

When I returned to Rigel's manor, I told him I had accepted the role. He thought for a moment with a conflicted look on his face.

"His Majesty is right. You would fit the role better than Galil."

"If I might ask, what exactly does a field marshal do?"

"Well, first off, you'll need to send for clothes worthy of the position." *True, clothes do maketh the man.* "I'll make the arrangements. But..." He trailed off, struggling with his next words.

"The cost?"

"Yes, I can foot the bill for armor, but formalwear worthy of your appointment ceremony is more than my salary can provide for. Luckily, you should get enough income out of Kadann Hill. I can make the down payment for now, so please pay the rest once you start bringing in an income."

That was apparently why I'd been given the territory. I couldn't just rely on others forever.

"Understood. I'll pay you back as soon as I can."

"Thank you. Oh, but I can supply a sword."

"Are you sure?"

"When a knight is invested, it is customary for their guardian to send a sword."

"Then I might take you up on that offer."

"Incidentally, Hero, do you have a crest of your own? A field marshal must have an armor and shield bearing his crest."

"I do. Do you have something to draw on?"

He brought me a sheet of parchment and a quill pen. I took them and drew the usual symbol.

"Hmm. A spring and a maiden, is it?"

It was a picture of a woman praying beside a small fountain. Ever since my first adventure, I would use that drawing whenever I needed a banner.

"Is there a problem? I'm not familiar with this world's customs."

"No, it should not be an issue. May I ask where it comes from?"

"I was saved by a water goddess, once upon a time."

"I see. It will make for a splendid crest."

In truth, the one I met was no goddess. She was just a girl. But the difference was inconsequential, as she was akin to a goddess in my eyes.

"Come to think of it, there was a strange old man in His Majesty's room. Who is he?"

"An old man by His Majesty's side? Are you talking about Fortogan?"

"I didn't get his name, but his eyes were sharp."

"Then there can be no doubt about it. I don't know too much about him either."

"Even you don't know?"

"Nobody does. Where he hails from is also a mystery. At the very least, he's not from any notable house. He's been hanging around His Majesty ever since the previous king passed away, though he rarely appears in public. When you do see him, he's often behind the king, whispering in his ear. Rumor has it His Majesty sees him as his prime confidant."

A mysterious confidant of dubious origins. I had painted a picture of him in my head, and the reality turned out to be a perfect match. Entirely enigmatic.

"Is it all right to let someone like that associate with the king?"

"There are various rumors, but look into any of them, and you'll find them completely baseless. He does not use his position to line his own pockets, nor does he side with any factions. Perhaps he's not actually a bad person."

Is that really okay? Perhaps Rigel was a bit too trusting. That may have been why His Majesty hadn't chosen him to be field marshal. Of course, who was I to talk about dubious origins? I was honestly just as shady.

"In fact, Hero, perhaps he's the one who advised His Majesty to appoint you."

I had a nightmare that night. The usual one, about the time I was brought back to reality from my first adventure. I woke up in the dream—opened my eyes to my own room. The room I had longed to return to.

As the nostalgia washed over me, I wept, knowing it had all been a dream. My mother flew into the room when she heard me sobbing. Then I awoke for real in this strange, fantastical world.

She hadn't seen me in half a year. For me, however, it was much longer.

CHAPTER 3

RAGING DRAGON VERALGON

THE NIGHT AFTER the reporting ceremony, there was a line of people waiting to greet me outside Rigel's estate. The most notable visitor, however, had already come first thing in the morning.

"It's a pleasure to make your acquaintance, Hero. My name is Romwell, and I am a servant of God."

The old man called Romwell wore plain priest clothes and had a peaceful, round face. I got the feeling I'd seen him before, but I couldn't remember where.

"It's been a while, head priest," Rigel said to him.

"No need to call me that. I came as nothing more than a believer wishing to meet God's messenger."

The head priest? Oh, the one who intimidated that bear-man at the ceremony. On closer inspection, that was definitely the face, but he gave off such a different aura that I still struggled to connect him with my memory.

"I apologize for never introducing myself. There was a series of intricate circumstances at play, and I never found the opportunity to pay you a visit," he said, lowering his head.

"Oh, no, I should have come to you. It is an honor to be personally visited by the head priest."

Once introductions were done, we chatted about a handful of inoffensive topics: whether my current lifestyle suited me, whether the food was to my tastes. After that, the head priest seemed to want to say something more important. His expression remained serene, but there was a slight nervousness in his eyes. It looked like we were getting close to the real purpose of his visit, but he kept holding his tongue.

"......"

He just couldn't seem to get started. He would open his mouth, then close it, then do it all over again—rinse and repeat. Apparently this was a topic that required a certain level of resolve. I already had a general idea of what it was.

I gave Rigel a look. He got the message.

"I've just remembered some business I have to attend to," he said. "If you'll excuse me. Ring the bell if you need me for anything."

I waited for the door to click shut behind him and then started the conversation myself.

"Is there something you want to ask me?"

The head priest took in a deep breath and then slowly opened his mouth. "Hero, have you ever met God?"

How very blunt of him. As I expected, it was a simple yet difficult question. Gods came in all shapes and sizes. In a few worlds, I'd met powerful entities claiming to be gods, but that likely wasn't what he was asking about.

I would need to choose my answer carefully. The last time I answered a similar question, I found myself pursued by fanatical assassins for days on end. Sure, I could take them out easily, but the lack of sleep really took a toll. In the end, an assassin disguised as a harlot slipped a dose of poison into her secret—never mind, let's not go there. That one was my fault for going around proclaiming half-truths in God's name. I was pretty unruly back then.

In any case, my answer to the question might crumble his faith and upend his entire worldview. I could see why he was so nervous.

I took another look at him. He was totally focused, doing his utmost not to miss a single word or change in my expression. While the look in his eyes was grimly serious, he seemed rational. In that case, it would be best to answer honestly. I had always been terrible at lying.

"By 'God,' do you mean the entity who sent me to this world?"

"Yes, I assume so."

That made this so much simpler.

"In that case, no, I have never met them. Nor have I ever heard their voice. I've only felt their presence. I can't even say for sure whether that entity is the same as the God you believe in. And, of course, I have not met your God either."

"Then you did not come from the Land of God?"

"No. The world I lived in was somewhat different from this one, but it was a world inhabited by humans. It was not a holy place." *Though to be fair, if he actually went and saw it, he might mistake it for God's domain.* "Back in my own world, I return to being a human without any special powers. I can only use my abilities as a hero when I'm sent to other worlds."

"Why were you chosen?"

"I don't know."

I didn't want to say this, but it had been merely a whim, as far as I knew. I didn't have any special talents to speak of.

"I see," he said, then held his silence for a bit. "Then you don't know anything about God."

"I do not."

I knew nothing about the one who had sent me either. I had no answers for the man, but he looked satisfied.

"Thank you for answering my impudent questions."

"I should be apologizing—I couldn't give any decent answers."

"That's not true at all. I believe I've learned something worthwhile. I would love to stay and chat longer, but unfortunately, I have mountains of busywork to attend to. Perhaps another day."

"Whenever you have the chance." *Oh, I almost forgot.* "Incidentally..."

"Is something the matter?"

"Should I answer the same way if anyone else asks about God?"

The head priest grinned. "In my estimation, you're a terrible liar. Those answers should suffice. You are proof that while he may take many forms, the might of our Great God reaches across other worlds entirely."

He held out his hand and I shook it. It was callused and

wrinkled, but warm. He rang the bell, gave his thanks to Rigel, and then left in the modest wagon he'd arrived in.

After his departure, I spent the rest of the morning dealing with the visitors who had formed a line of their own accord. I'd hear their names, exchange a few words, then excuse them. It was practically an idol handshake session. Though I told them we would "talk again," I could hardly remember all their names.

"That's not a problem. There wasn't a single one worth remembering," said Garlo, the palace's etiquette teacher.

After he'd finished teaching me how to behave at the reporting ceremony, he stuck around to teach me the proper manners of this world. *Not that that excuses his tone.*

"They're already used to being treated like that," he added. "Even if you don't remember their names, just act as if you know them, and they'll play along."

That's supposed to be good manners?

"But knowing I might see them later, wouldn't I be better off asking for their names again?"

"In that case, you would be disgracing them. If you disgrace them so obviously, the wounded party won't be able to let it go. Even if they knew that it would get them killed, they might draw their swords in order to save face. If you absolutely must ask them, please do so casually, in a place where no one can see you."

Was that really how this society worked? How barbaric. Though I had to admit, my world had been like that once upon a time, and many others were no different.

'|X|'

The seemingly unending line of visitors cleared up by lunchtime. Garlo explained that it was considered rude to visit people in the afternoon unless you were invited or unless you were close family.

Most of the visitors came with gifts. I wanted to return the favor, but Garlo simply shuffled the gifts up, matched value and status, and then regifted them back. *I guess that counts?* He continued to insist I didn't need to remember anyone, despite the fact that he clearly knew who every single one of them was.

Of course, unlike me, Garlo had lived his whole life in this world. He'd likely known all of them for a long time. Even so, handling guests in those numbers was quite an achievement. *I would love to keep his services even after the lessons are over.*

Quite a few of the visitors came with requests for me. "Someone's trying to illegally inherit my territory," "A neighboring lord is using our lord's absence to his advantage," and so on. The last one was "As the field marshal, please annihilate them. Or at least give the order..."

I didn't want to carelessly stick my nose into these matters. I might have earned a few favors, but I'd create grudges as well. The requests all came from the houses whose heads and firstborn sons were lost in the last battle. His Majesty's—or perhaps the sharp-eyed man's—suspicions were on the mark.

"Please have His Majesty weigh in on these matters," I said. "If anyone disagrees with his decisions, then I'll take care of them."

I was appointed field marshal to keep the military completely out of civil affairs—to prevent a civil war from breaking out. To that end, I was not going to make any decisions. I was going to pass them all on to His Majesty.

No, I am not shirking my duties. That is my strategy, and I'm sticking to it.

What had always worked for me so far was to keep my nose out of each world's business as much as possible. I knew what would happen if I got too involved. If I kept charging at every problem that presented itself, I'd end up aimlessly spinning my wheels forever. I would gain allies, and I would make enemies, in an endless cycle. I would be worn ragged before the world was saved. So if the world could be saved without interfering in human squabbles, that was how I would do it.

A few were making another type of request too.

"My husband's (or son's, or master's, or relative's) army is stranded on the other side of the mountains. Could you please drive away the army at the gates and save them?"

As I recalled, close to three thousand were stranded. If we saved them, three thousand would be added to our own forces. And if the feudal lords returned, that might help stabilize the situation. If it worked out, some would be in debt to me, but it wouldn't attract resentment from others. At present, no one knew if those marooned armies were still alive. I decided I'd consult Rigel.

"If I want to gather the lords' armies to save the forces trapped across the mountains, what should I do first?"

"That's a difficult question." Rigel seemed conflicted. "First, you're not a field marshal until the ceremony. After the ceremony, you'll have the power to issue a summons. But few lords will answer it. Optimistically, you would command a quarter of the forces we possessed in the previous battle."

"So few, eh?"

"With this and that, quite a few won't send their armies. We were only able to gather so many last time because of how people felt about the princess. Many of those loyal to the royal line were lost in the war. Those who are left are working hard to rebuild what they've lost. They won't send out soldiers when they can hardly support themselves."

I see.

"You're saying I can't count on the lords."

"Correct."

"Do we have any other powers?"

Rigel thought for a few moments, groaning to himself, and then talked me through the possibilities. "First, you have my dragon riders. Unfortunately, they won't be of much use until the dragons return. That's only a matter of time. The royal guard is meant to protect His Majesty, so even a field marshal cannot command them. The same goes for the garrison stationed at Dragonjaw Gate. They won't move from their position, no matter who gives the order."

"What about the Knights Templar? The temple's forces?"

"I presume that if the hero gives the order, they will assemble at once, even before you're officially field marshal. However, they were essentially annihilated, you see... The talent for magic is rare. The plan is to eventually elevate the trainees to proper knights, but who knows whether they'll be useful? It will take at least ten years for the Knights Templar to regain their original power."

Yes, Liana said something similar.

"Other than that... You might be able to gather a few mercenaries and free knights. But you'll have to foot the costs yourself. There's a limit to how many you can afford to hire."

The conclusion was unavoidable: There were no armies, save for Rigel's dragon riders, that I could rely on. And they couldn't move just yet.

His explanation ended with a sigh. "God finally sent us a hero, yet we can hardly do a thing for him. Pathetic."

"It's not your fault. If you could have solved your problems without me, I would not have been summoned to this world." Although I was trying to console him, I was disappointed by how little they could offer. "How long until the dragons return?"

"If I had to guess, they should be back in ten days."

Ten days. Ten days before I could use the only forces at my disposal. Now, what would I do until then?

†|¤|†

The next day, I told Rigel I wanted to see a map, and for some reason, he took me to the dragon house. This was a dragon breeding ground about an hour's ride from the capital. It was the base of operations for the dragon riders, located on a plateau the size of a baseball field that jutted out on the west side of Dragonbone Ridge. There were simple walls on either side, lined with the statues of most peculiar beasts. Like the capital, the eastern side pressed against the steep mountains, where an unbelievably large dragon statue was carved into the bare rock face.

"What you see there is the flight platform. The dragons use it to take flight." Rigel pointed to the west, where there was a grass-covered plaza. Its western edge dropped off abruptly into nothingness. "This area always receives a steady westward wind. It is the perfect place to fly a dragon."

As if supporting Rigel's words, a flag fluttered gently in the direction of the steep drop-off. Hoisted over the simple observation deck in the northwest corner, it bore the crest of the dragon riders.

"What we're looking for is over there." He turned toward the giant statue. A clean semicircular hole at its feet led into a long tunnel even wider than the entrance.

The cave was about twenty meters across and five hundred meters deep. There were forty holes on each side of the passage, each leading to a smaller chamber. Though less perfectly shaped, each chamber was still the size of a cozy house.

"This is the dragons' den, although it's currently vacant."

Inside the vast cave, people who must have been the dragon caretakers wandered around, cleaning and looking generally bored. They seemed kind of spaced out, like nothing they were doing really mattered. *Perhaps that's why the space feels so needlessly vast. Even so, imagine how much time it must have taken to dig all this out and carve that giant statue at the entrance.*

"It's quite spacious. Is this also a remnant of ancient magic?"

"Not exactly. It's said that this cave existed before our ancestors came to these lands. According to legend, clever children with beards once called this place their home."

Bearded children... Does he mean dwarves?

"Are those children still around?"

"They don't exist outside of folklore."

So dwarves are already extinct. What a drab world.

"However it came to be, we currently use it to rear dragons. Dragons in the wild make their nests in stone caves." He pointed at one of the misshapen rooms, explaining that those had been excavated by humans. "We house seventy-two at the moment. This year was a breeding year, so perhaps we'll have a few more infants by this time next year. We'll have to wait another ten years before they're ready for battle."

We proceeded deeper as I listened to his explanations. My eyes came to rest on a chamber that was quite a bit bigger than the others. The hole was packed full of what looked like straw. It was probably fodder, but for whom? The stables were down below the cliffs. Horses were afraid of dragons, so they couldn't house them next to each other—and that was why we were forced to climb here on foot. My point was that horse feed would not be stored here.

Do the dragons eat it, then? I'd never seen vegetarian dragons in the other worlds, although there was no reason they shouldn't exist somewhere.

"That's smithing grass," Rigel explained, noticing my gaze. "It burns hot enough to melt iron. All the capital's smiths use it in their forges. Dragons eat it to breathe fire. It was once said, 'He who controls Dragon Peak controls the kingdom,' and that is because smithing grass only grows on that mountain. It's why the dragons flock to it. A dragon who can't breathe fire is not much of a threat."

I had to wonder about that, but I knew I would be on the receiving end of a long story if I opened my mouth, so I just let it slide. To the old man, dragon riders were most valuable for their ability to vaporize the enemy lines with their flames, and he did have a point.

At the back of the cave was a stone doorway protected by two monstrous statues. The doors were embedded with nine gemstones, each different in color and shape. On Rigel's urging, I tried giving them a push, but they didn't budge. Once more, I tried with my hero's power, to no avail. Just in case, I tried pulling, but the result was the same.

"It opens when you touch the stones in the right order." He demonstrated, and the door opened without a sound.

"Is this the work of those bearded children?"

"So I've been told. It seems even the temple scholars don't understand how it works."

The passage beyond the door, while not as vast as the one we'd been walking through so far, was still quite spacious. Each side was lined with doors at regular intervals.

"There are contraptions like these scattered all over the ruins.

We are only making use of a small portion of the site. Once upon a time, a group of bored youngsters went on a search and found a silver sword in the deepest parts. But perhaps some got lost, as not all of them returned. Now then, this is the room."

He pushed open a large set of doors at the end of the passage that opened into a dome. In addition to the entrance, there were eleven doors systematically spaced around it, and in the center, a waist-high circular platform around ten meters in diameter.

My eyes were drawn to something above the platform.

"Is this...a map?"

"Correct."

Perhaps it would be more accurate to use the word "model." The coasts, the mountains, the rivers, and the seas were all carved in three dimensions. I had been wondering why we had to go so far just to see a map, but it was certainly impressive enough to warrant the trip.

"It must have been made in ancient times. Some of the rivers don't match their current courses. However, everything else should match the actual geography."

"Is it oriented correctly too?"

"It should be," Rigel said, turning ninety degrees clockwise to face north. "Here is Dragonbone Ridge. Everything contained here is human domain." He picked up a long stick from the platform and used it to point out a nearby mountain range. As if it had been formed from a crater, a portion of the west side was dominated by a bay that was circular as well. The whole region was shaped like a crescent moon.

Our territory seemed to be on the northern tip of the continent—though much of the continent itself stretched beyond the southern rim of the platform, so I couldn't know its shape. The map only depicted a small part of the world. Sadly, the Dragonbone Ridge that sheltered humanity occupied only three meters of it on this model—no more than a tenth of the full surface.

"It's said that Dragonbone Ridge was formed from the remains of a great wyrm that threatened the world."

Yes, I guess I can sort of see it.

"And here is Dragon Peak. The royal capital is at its base."

He pointed out a conspicuously large mountain in the southeast region. There was a small model of a palace at its base. On closer inspection, I saw that the model contained other man-made structures—small castles and towns here and there. Representing only the most important places, they had been added by humans after the fact and were a bit cruder than the rest of the map. I spotted what I presumed to be the model for Dragonjaw Gate on the southern rim.

Rigel pointed out a slit in the mountains on the north side directly opposite the capital. "Over here is Chezarith Castle," he said. "It's the farthest castle from the capital. It would take a dragon at least two days to get there, depending on the weather."

That comparison may have been clear for him, but I had yet to ride any of the world's dragons, so it meant nothing to me.

"How long would it take by horse?" I asked.

"Hmm... A horse? Now how long *would* that take..." Rigel cocked his head and thought. He had likely never traveled to the castle by horse. "Come to think of it, Galeom—he's the lord there—said it was a twenty-day journey from his territory to the capital. It's around six days by ship from Port Corcalla and then another fourteen days from the port to the capital. Though that includes some walking."

"I see."

I tried roughly calculating the distance by travel time but gave up when my head started hurting. I didn't know how fast ships went and wasn't even sure that a day was twenty-four hours here, though my internal clock told me it was somewhere in the same ballpark.

Distances aside, I now understood that twenty days from end to end was the breadth of the world, as far as its humans were concerned.

I remembered that those two bumbling buffoons in *Tokaidochu Hizakurige*—an old travel guide—took around thirteen days on foot to get from Edo to Osaka. With that in mind, this world was pretty small. Of course, the *world* was far wider than that, but everything outside those mountains was off limits to humans.

Rigel continued explaining parts of the map, but I wasn't expecting to remember any of it. Once I got back to the manor, I would have to borrow a more reasonably sized map to review.

All of a sudden, a model on the opposite side of the platform caught my eye.

"What's that?"

"Oh, that? That's the old capital. It's said that humanity lived there, once upon a time. That's where the road out of Dragonjaw Gate eventually leads."

"There used to be human territory beyond the mountains?"

"Yes, according to old legends. Though they're such a distant memory, I couldn't tell you how long ago that was."

"You mean those ruins are the stuff of legends?"

"No, the ruins exist. That's for sure. I myself participated in an expedition to the old capital in my youth."

Ruins of the ancients. Now that sounds interesting. "I'd love to see it."

"That might prove a bit difficult."

"Why's that?"

"The old capital takes many days to reach, even by dragon. You will have no choice but to land and rest along the way. Back in my youth, most of the orcs still lived far to the south—there were few of them in the northern regions. It was possible to head south from here unnoticed. But now, that isn't possible. Their settlements stretch all the way to the base of Dragonbone Ridge. In all likelihood, you would be attacked in your sleep. Even back then, we had to fly the last few days nonstop if we wanted to reach the old capital safely. Sure, as the hero, you might be able to turn the tables on them, but if a surprise attack takes out your dragon's wings, that's as far as you go."

Meaning that the orcs had progressed immensely in just one generation. Honestly, what was I supposed to do about it?

Southwest of Dragonjaw Gate.

Clay, son of Arlay, peeked carefully out of the dense forest. His stomach growled. He'd last eaten over three days ago, and what he was feeling transcended hunger. There was a prickling pain in his guts, and his throat was parched. Only when he was asleep could he forget his body's demands.

Looking up at the sky, Clay confirmed the position of the sun. Its height hadn't changed much from when he last checked. It would still be quite a while before he could swap shifts with someone else. *"We'll all starve to death if we can't break through! In that case, we'd be better off fighting to the last!"*

Those words had been spoken by the man who had been his employer up to a few days ago—who had then followed them to the letter. Those words had been his last.

Clay was a free knight and survivor of a battle with one of the subjugation forces stranded outside the mountains. The unit he'd offered his services to had gone around making a mess of various orc settlements, claiming an abundance of spoils of war. The gains had been greater than ever recently, so even a hired hand like Clay could expect a substantial reward.

However, upon his triumphant return to Dragonjaw Gate, he came face-to-face with the legions of orcs blocking the valley. The commander of the subjugation unit was too proud to turn back and attempted to force his way through. The rest was history.

Luckily, that foolish commander had charged at the vanguard and was the first to be taken. Those in the rear, including Clay, made an about-face the instant that their leader fell and somehow made a successful retreat. Even so, they paid quite a price. More than half the knights of the subjugation force—the most gallant and brave ones at that—perished in battle. They had lost their warpriests and foot soldiers, and their wagons as well. Naturally, it also cost them their mountain of spoils.

Now the longest-serving free knights were rallying the remnants together. There were only forty of them left. These last few days had been miserable. Without food or shelter, they were tormented by hunger and cold as they spent their days cowering from orcish pursuit.

Perhaps that man was right, Clay thought as he held his stomach. Those who died in battle went to the Warriors' Garden. No doubt his employer was eating his fill in the garden right now. But where did those who'd starved end up?

A shrill screech dragged him back to reality, and Clay's vision was filled with the sight of a terrifying beast. It had a wolf-like build with an ominous beak—an orc on its back. *Bloody beak-dogs!* They were the only cavalry the orcs possessed. And of them all, the platoon led by the Black Dog was the very symbol of fear for those in the subjugation forces.

He could see ten of them. The orcs had come to a stop a short distance from the forest, and luckily, they didn't seem to have noticed him yet.

Clay retreated cautiously, taking care not to make a sound. He needed to inform his comrades in the forest.

The old knight he reported to immediately woke the others and ordered them to prepare for battle, then followed Clay to the forest's outskirts. When they both carefully peeked out of the thicket, they saw that the orcs had dismounted and were taking a break. It looked like they were about to have lunch.

Clay gulped as his eyes honed in on the bread and dried meat in their hands. The old knight tugged him by the sleeve and pointed out a particular orc. He had only one eye and was petting the head of a black beak-dog. *Right, an orc with one eye. Exactly as the rumors described him.* Clay gulped again, for different reasons this time.

It was him. The Black Dog.

"Back to camp," the old knight whispered. Clay nodded awkwardly and followed, his legs trembling beneath him.

When they returned to their comrades, the old knight growled an order.

"The Black Dog is here. We're taking him out." Every face filled with fear, but the knight paid them no mind. "We're up against twelve beak-dogs. They are presumably the enemy's advance force, but they haven't noticed us yet. They've let their guards down and are taking a carefree break right under our noses."

He looked at all the gathered faces before continuing.

"The enemy is few in number. If we launch a surprise attack now, we will undoubtedly win. There is great significance in crushing their advance force. They will grow more cautious. Their pursuit will be slower." Then he grinned. "Did I mention they're eating? Why don't we nab ourselves a bite?"

His call to arms was met with growling stomachs. Everyone laughed in hushed tones.

With a satisfied smile, the old knight mounted his horse. "The Black Dog's head is ours. It will be a small battle, but it will be spoken of for generations to come. Now, all hands, move out!"

The starving knights followed his lead.

The orcs noticed them the instant they burst out of the forest. As expected of the Black Dog's platoon, they reacted in a flash, throwing their meals down on the spot, leaping atop their beak-dogs, and fleeing without a second glance.

Their mounts were slightly faster than horses. They gained distance, bit by bit.

"After them! Chase them down!" the old knight screamed. "That's the Black Dog! He's at the front!"

The orc riders turned to face backward on their saddles and fired their guns. Dust clouds burst all around the old knight as he took the lead. An unlucky comrade beside Clay took a shot to his horse and fell. Clay didn't look back to watch him go. By now, the enemies' backs were all he could see.

While the orcs' mounts were faster, the knights' horses had more stamina. The beak-dogs were already slowing little by little. Clay's platoon would eventually catch up and kill them—as long as they didn't flee into the forest.

They chased the beak-dogs over a hill, where a plain of tall grass spread out a short distance ahead. The Black Dog made a dash straight for it.

Fool. Do you think you can hide in there? We'll hunt you down.

The corners of Clay's lips curled up. They were gaining on the orcs with every bound. They'd just need one last burst of speed.

But right before they reached the grass, the beak-dogs leapt high into the air.

What?

Suddenly, the grass breathed flames. The old knight fell from his horse. The surrounding knights were knocked off their mounts one after the next, or toppled along with them.

The grass burst with fire again.

It's an ambush, he realized. But it was too late. The ground rose to meet him—he had fallen with his horse. He tried to ignore the pain and stand, but his right foot was caught in the stirrup. He wrenched his body away. *There isn't a second to spare—I have to get out of here.* But it was futile. A comrade who had managed to turn around in time raced past him in the opposite direction. He was about to plead for help when a bullet took the man out.

A separate unit of beak-dogs had already circled around behind them. The remaining knights were surrounded.

Orc foot soldiers marching in single file appeared from the thicket ahead with long spears in hand. They were closely followed by gunmen, who had finished reloading. From time to time, they would stop to stab the finishing blow into a fallen knight before advancing again.

There was no hope of survival now.

On that day, Clay, son of Arlay, set off for the Warriors' Garden.

The Black Dog gazed up at the army of helmets piled up in the camp at the entrance to the valley. It was a symbol of the spoils they had gained in the previous battles, and the cleanup that followed.

Some barely counted as helmets—little more than pots with string tied to the handles—but there were still close to ten thousand in total. Soon, they would be transported to the margrave's capital, where they would be made into a tangible monument to the spoils of war. His ancestors once brought the heads of enemies home to boast of their achievements, but that barbarous custom had gone out of style. Anyone who tried that nowadays would be more disdained than respected. He needed to be cautious; there was already deep-seated prejudice against his plan. One wrong step, and he would be treated as a monster. Even if it *was* humans he was fighting.

Irritated, the Black Dog delivered a sharp kick to a helmet that had tumbled off the pile. The wound in his side throbbed. The helmet smacked hard into the mountain, then bounced back with a terrible clamor and found its way back to his feet. The head of a boar with bared tusks sneered up at him. It looked identical to the margrave's lazy son, who commanded the margrave's army.

He was completely incompetent, with indolence being his sole defining feature. In fact, his greatest accomplishment had been essentially punting his command duties to the Black Dog and his men. *Just as well. If that man had actually opened his mouth, nothing good would have come out of it.*

If this had been an opportunity for the Black Dog to make a name for himself, that would have been different. However, the fellow was not called the "lazy son" for nothing. He had claimed nearly all the Black Dog's accomplishments as his own. *He only moves cleverly when it comes to such vile misdeeds.* In the end, all the margrave's public praise—and all the medals from the Assembly—had gone to that imbecile.

Of course, everyone knew whom that victory truly belonged to. The margrave's soldiers knew, and so did the margrave himself. That old orc who ruled the northernmost border had been his patron, lifting up the Black Dog—no more than a mercenary from the southern tribe—and making him an executive in his army. He rated the Black Dog especially highly and had privately sent him praise, money, and an apology for the public disregard. He also scolded him for allowing himself to be wounded, but that was out of genuine concern.

Even so, the Black Dog felt slighted.

He kicked the helmet again. This time, he kicked it away from the mountain, and it didn't come back.

So be it, he whispered to himself. *I'll get another chance. I still have control over the margrave's army. Though he doesn't have much time left.*

The Black Dog loathed the idea of growing famous under the lazy son's reign after the margrave passed away. Thus, he needed to develop his reputation as much as he could before that happened.

One of his men came to report that the preparations were complete. On the Black Dog's signal, a line of large ox-drawn wagons started to move. The margrave had pleaded for their loan from the empire's main army, and they had arrived just the other day. While the Black Dog normally preferred something more agile, they would be the most effective tool to break through the current predicament.

At the end of his sights, the head of a massive carved water dragon glared at him and his men from the depths of the valley.

'|X|'

"Hero! Hero!"

The voice came from nowhere in particular. *Where am I? Oh, right. It's my thirteenth world. I was sent here to save it.*

I mustered my motivation and endeavored to drag myself back to consciousness.

My vision swimming, I imagined I saw a white robe-like vestment. Just like the ones she used to wear.

"It's too early to run out of strength!"

But it wasn't her voice I heard. It was an old man. My mind began to fade away again.

Bang! An impact rattled my brain. The pain rapidly brought me to my senses. Before my eyes stood a scowling, bald-headed priest holding a staff that looked like a large pestle. He claimed that it was an ancient and honorable staff that was permitted to smack any head, even if that head belonged to the king.

"I don't have all the time in the world. I'm here because I got a request from the hero himself."

"I-I'm sorry. I'm not sleepy anymore, so please go on."

He let out a deep sigh before returning his eyes to the book-stand. His monotonous voice picked up where it had left off reading from an oversized and splendidly ornamented book of vellum paper.

"And that year, Elron was blessed with his fifth son from his third wife. The child was named Wargan, and once he grew, he wed the daughter of Gauls to be blessed with four sons, but eventually, the first two would fall in the war with Berion; the third son drove off the fourth and became the protector of the clan. He himself would wed the daughters of the first son and have his sons wed the daughters of the fourth. Once the family was united once more, on the first moon of the year of fire-moons, Wargan raised an army. To combat this, Berion joined forces with Verdemoth, son of Gauls, and met them on the plains of Morlang. It was an intense clash of armies. The battle lasted three days and three nights, while the plains were covered in bodies and blood. In the words of those days, Morlang meant the *blood bog*. It was Wargan who eventually came out on top, and after severing each of Berion's limbs, he buried them deep and far from one another. He buried the torso right where it was slain and displayed the head at his own manor. Verdemoth became a prisoner of war, although he was eventually treated as a guest. The next year, he fell to illness..."

It had been my idea to study history. While the field marshal appointment ceremony had gone off without a hitch, the dragons had yet to return. I thought I might learn about this world in my free time.

History is important. It tells of how the world came to be, the standing of each power, the characteristics of each region, and the ethical traditions, among other things. But despite everything there was to learn, my mind could not keep up. Whomever had sent me to this world had not enhanced my brain. This was the problem every time, and I was all too often reminded of my own stupidity.

The man presenting the lecture was a scholar who was the king's very own tutor. I knew I shouldn't complain when I was the one who made the request, but I was starting to wonder if the problem lay in his teaching style. His lesson consisted of nothing more than reciting from a history book. There was no question-and-answer involved.

It would be better if I did the reading myself, I thought. But when I asked for the book, my request was curtly denied.

"That is forbidden," he told me.

Apparently, anyone who did not have the qualifications of a scholar— even including the king—was forbidden from touching the temple's books. *Books must be a priceless commodity here after all. Still, if this is how it's going to be, perhaps I'd be better off hiring a minstrel. My knowledge of history might turn out rather biased, but it wouldn't be so boring.*

Suddenly, the door flew open and Rigel entered, a look of joy on his face. It was rare to see that earnest man wearing such an expression—in fact, this was the first time I'd ever seen it.

"Do you have good news?" I asked.

"The dragons are back!"

Oh, that's very good news.

"Let's go see them at once! I have a horse for you!"

He pulled me out of the room without waiting for a reply. I looked back to see the abandoned scholar preparing to leave, expressionless.

We reached the dragon rider HQ twice as fast as last time—Rigel had the horses galloping at full speed practically the whole way. As we left the horses at the stable at the bottom of the hill, a massive shadow passed overhead. I looked up to see a dragon touching down on the cliff.

Oh...that's rare.

We arrived up top to find the dragon surrounded by its keepers. One dragon keeper was thrusting out a long stick to attract the dragon's attention, and while it was distracted, the others parted its plumage to check up on something.

"The dragons here have feathers, I see."

"Are they different in other worlds?" Rigel looked at me, perplexed.

"Yes, that's right. I've seen fourteen worlds, this one included, and seven of them had dragons. Only one other world had feathered dragons."

What's more, those feathered dragons were a special breed that dwelled in the mountains of the north. The other dragons of that world had scales. *Ah, perhaps it's the same here. Maybe the south has naked dragons.*

This dragon was between five and six meters in size. In silhouette, it resembled a tyrannosaurus, but its entire body was covered in richly colored feathers, and instead of forelimbs, it boasted a massive pair of wings. In contrast to the bright colors that caught the eye at first glance, its underbelly was an ashen gray.

The keeper with the stick wrapped its end in several layers of cloth and then dunked it into a barrel. Once the cloth was thoroughly soaked in whatever liquid it contained, he placed it where the other keepers were indicating. I could see a faint red tint. It seemed they were trying to apply some salve to an injury.

The instant the shaft touched its wound, the dragon started to thrash about. It flailed its long tail at the keeper, but he easily dodged, seeming quite practiced. The other keepers raised warnings as they stepped away, taking the ropes from their belts and swinging them around. I saw that there were loops at the ends of the ropes. *They're practically cowboys.*

They threw the ropes in unison, but the dragon brushed them all aside.

"He probably fought over a female dragon in the mountains. Most of the dragons are injured when they return from breeding seasons. They need treatment, but they're pretty rowdy for a short period after they return. This is when the dragon keepers have the most trouble."

Rigel's voice was as level as ever. This had to be a common occurrence.

The dragon roared, baring its sharp fangs to intimidate the keepers. They threw their ropes again, and this time, a young keeper managed to get his rope around its neck. The others rushed to help, but before they could, the dragon swung its muscular neck, sending the young keeper flying through the air and crashing into another keeper.

Now their coordination was thrown off. The man on the floor, who must have been leading the effort, barked instructions from the ground, but the others hesitated. The dragon swung its tail again, knocking another keeper off his feet.

"Oh, that's not good!" Rigel raced off to help, and a number of dragon riders rushed out of the cave.

I considered following him, but I had no idea how to handle the situation and thought I might just incur the dragon's wrath. I didn't know how dangerous this world's dragons were, but I decided to stay where I was.

After a struggle, Rigel managed to straddle the rampaging dragon. He stroked it, and it immediately grew docile and was lured into the cave by its keepers. Three keepers came out of the effort with broken bones, while Rigel took a few strikes and some light burns.

Rigel returned with a bitter smile, saying, "I'm sorry you had to see that." After he got a bit of first aid, I followed him into the cave.

One third of the caverns were already occupied; the rest of the dragons would be back in two or three days. There were keepers busily running about, and unlike last time, they were brimming with energy.

"This is Greilgon, my trusty steed." Rigel introduced me to an emerald-green dragon with vivid red flight feathers. Like the other dragon, its lower half was light gray. I could tell it was fluffy just by looking at it.

"Could I touch him?"

"He's a calm one. You should be all right."

Great. I fluffed him up. *Oh...how soft, warm...and splendid.*

"I knew it. You have the talent."

"Talent?"

"Indeed. The talent to convey your thoughts to dragons. Anyone who doesn't have it can't ride."

"How can you tell?"

"Dragons hate to be touched by those without talent. At times, they'll bite them to death if they get too close."

He could have told me that earlier.

"Then I'm able to ride dragons?"

"The talent itself isn't that rare. I'd estimate around one out of every ten people can touch dragons. The keepers are all selected from those with talent. That said, very few can handle them as freely as a dragon rider. It depends on your affinity with the dragon too."

I see.

"Would you like to try it out?"

Rigel led me to another chamber. The reddish-brown dragon stretched out there was so elderly that its age was obvious even to a layman. For some reason, its eyes felt gentler than the others'. Rigel pointed at the base of its wings.

"Try touching it there."

He's not going to fly into a rage, is he?

"What happens if someone without the right talent does it?"

"They will be killed."

Well, I'm glad I asked.

"Don't worry. I can already tell you have a certain level of talent. He's always been a gentle soul, so it won't be that terrible."

I took a deep breath and reached out.

The dragon showed absolutely no reaction when I touched it. *Was that really the right spot?*

"Looks like you're in the clear. I expect no less from a hero. The rest is a matter of compatibility."

Hmm, apparently, I have the talent to be a dragon rider. Or perhaps it was simply the effect of my hero powers.

"How do we determine compatibility?"

"That's something only trial and error can reveal. First, you should learn to fly on Igergon here. I was taught to fly on him too. Come to think of it, have you ever ridden dragons in other worlds?"

"Yes, but only once. I've ridden eagles and griffons too."

The dragon I rode was covered in hard scales, could communicate with telepathy, and had mastered the art of magic. To be honest, it was more accurate to say he let me sit on his back.

"In that case, you might pick it up quickly. The most important thing is to form a bond with your dragon—"

Suddenly, we heard some kind of disturbance outside of the cage. An old man, likely a keeper, ran up.

"Captain Rigel! Big trouble!"

"What's wrong?"

"It's Veralgon! He's back! He'll be touching down soon!"

"What?!"

Rigel's face turned grim. "Keep the young ones out of it," he said. "We'll need seasoned hands."

"Yes, sir!"

The old man ran quickly out of the cave again. "Get Rhayner and Gadoss!" Rigel called to the attendants who followed him and was about to leave as well when he suddenly turned to me.

"Hero, you..." He paused. "You come with me."

Outside of the cave, a lone dragon was beating its wings as it slowly descended. It was around twice the size of the other dragons; pure white except for eyes that glimmered a fiery, ruby-like crimson. There wasn't a single bloodstain on its pristine plumage. That was proof of its overwhelming strength. The keepers drew closer to make sure, looking nervous as could be.

The white dragon roared. The air quivered, and everyone who heard it froze in place. This white monster lorded over all the humans frozen in its domain.

Our eyes met. I could feel a chill run down my spine. Its red eyes took me in.

"Rigel." I addressed the old man without taking my eyes off the dragon. "Can I have him?"

"Wh-what are you talking about?! Even an experienced dragon rider can't—"

A keeper standing behind the white dragon quietly removed a rope from his belt and prepared to throw it. The dragon noticed him and spun around, and that was my moment.

"H-hero! Wait—oh, fine! Everyone, support him!"

Although its back was turned toward me, its long tail flew at me like a well-aimed whip. I abruptly fell to my knees to dodge it. A *swoosh* flew past my ears as that white whirlwind passed over my head.

The keepers all threw their ropes at once, distracting the dragon for the briefest instant, and I dashed out again. Dodging the kick it unleashed with its sharp talons, I slipped under its stomach.

Twice, three times it tried to crush me underfoot. But I was in its blind spot, and it missed. As the white dragon roared in irritation, I seized my chance—jumping up, I latched onto its neck. It swung its head viciously, trying to cast me away. All I could do was hold on—it was impossible to even attempt to clamber onto its back.

All of a sudden, the dragon lurched back and froze. In the instant of stillness, I let go of its neck to reach toward its back, but before I could grab hold, it started bucking wildly, throwing me to the ground. I twisted and thrust my body sideways as it smacked its whole underside into the ground, raising a tremor in its wake.

Now the dragon's head came at me in a flash. I dodged it by rolling away into a stand, but just as I was up on my feet, I was struck by a wing. It was only a glancing blow, but taken by surprise, I was knocked off balance and thrown to the ground once more. Before I could react, a jaw lined with sharp fangs came at me. Just in time, I managed to roll to the side and narrowly avoid it.

"Now! Capture him!"

On that call, the many dragon keepers who had gathered during my struggle threw their ropes at once. The white dragon jerked back to brush them away, but two of the ropes managed to catch the claws on its wings.

The other keepers hurried to help the ones who had hit their mark, but the white dragon was too fast for them. The keeper who'd caught its left wing let go of the rope, realizing that help wouldn't arrive in time, but the other wasn't ready to give up. He clung to the rope and was flung about as the dragon twisted its body, knocking over the keepers who were rushing to the man's aid as he sailed through the air.

Suddenly, the perfect opportunity presented itself as the dragon turned away from me. I ran up to it and, before it could react, leapt upon its back.

As long as I clung to its back, the dragon couldn't reach to attack me, so while the strength of my grip held out, he was stuck with me. But now I realized: What was I supposed to do next? I had rushed out on the spur of the moment and stupidly had forgotten to ask the most important question. How was I supposed to get a dragon to listen to me?

I locked eyes with Rigel, my expression pleading for help.

"Hero!" he answered. "Hold down the base of its wings! You must have a conversation with its heart and win it over!"

What was that supposed to mean? How was I supposed to talk to it when it was in such a frenzy? The white dragon had begun thrashing to try to shake me off. Even if I wanted to, now I couldn't dismount without risking injury. I had no choice but to try.

First, the base of its wings. I clung to the dragon with all my might and carefully reached out with my right hand. Unfortunately, no matter how stretched, I was about a head's length short.

"Hero! Get down at once!" Rigel's warning rocked my ears.

What was it? I looked around. Suddenly, the white dragon spread its wings and began to run at a speed unthinkable for its massive body. Its eyes locked on to the sheer cliff—the takeoff platform. By the time I realized what it was trying to do, it was already too late. Its white bulk sprang into the open air with wings spread wide.

Gravity vanished. The dragon went into freefall—with me on its back. I thought we would plummet to the earth below us, but that feeling only lasted for an instant. Its spread wings immediately caught the wind, and we began to glide.

Higher and higher it climbed, beating its wings as if it had forgotten I was there. I used the opportunity to climb up to the base of its wings. My hands found their goal at exactly the moment that the white dragon shifted from ascent to nosedive.

My heart sank. Gravity was gone once more, and the ground approached at a breakneck pace. Touching the base of the dragon's wings, I made a prayer. *I don't care how you do it! Just calm down!* But the dragon rejected it. Yet, while I had been rejected, I felt it: I had brushed up against the dragon's soul. Using that feeling of rejection as my point of reference, I wished even harder. The white dragon resisted me at every turn. Then harder, harder still.

The dragon finally gave in.

PLANET OF THE ORCS

A new sensation was added to my five senses. My vision blurred to twofold. I quickly realized I was sharing the dragon's eyes. I could feel the heavy air sliding over its wings.

Before I realized what was happening, the ground filled my entire field of vision, but right before we collided with it, the dragon spread its wings and curved upward, snaking back toward the sky. Gravity returned, pressing my body against the white feathers of its back. Just like that, the earth was left behind, replaced by a blue sky as far as the eye could see. For a moment, the sun scorched my eyes, but then it too was gone as the dragon continued its circle of flight.

As we tilted around, belly skyward, there were no longer any forces holding me down. The inverted horizon came into view, but I flipped over just before it could center, returning the upside-down heavens to their rightful position. With one deep breath, I looked around.

I could see three hundred and sixty degrees—there was nothing to obstruct my view. The ground was so distant now. The only sound came from those white wings slicing through the wind.

I could feel my body lift as one wing caught an updraft. Without a moment's delay, we were swiveling left. I tried plunging the left wing into the updraft to return myself to level, but the air fought against it, and the tilt only grew worse. I instead angled the wings carefully to catch the draft with both.

We spun on the spot, finely adjusting to stay in that column of air. Once both wings had taken to it completely, we began gaining more and more altitude. With every new revolution, the world below grew farther and farther away. Sure, I could flap to ascend, but it was far easier just to catch a draft.

When I looked down, the now-minuscule dragon house caught my eye. Rigel and the dragon keepers were looking up at me, worried. Perhaps I had taken things a little too far. It was time to return. I angled the wings, escaping the column of air, spinning lazy circles as we began our descent.

My connection with the dragon was severed the moment we hit the ground. It started with my sight, then the sensation in my body, and then I was left all on my own. While I had simply been returned to my original state, my body was assailed by a peculiar sensation, feeling as if it had lost an integral piece.

"Hero! Are you all right?!" Rigel ran up to me. "How reckless can you be?! Without any saddle or reins, and it had to be Veralgon of all dragons! Think before you act!"

"I'm sorry. I just felt like I *had* to ride this dragon."

I knew that was no excuse. But if I answered honestly, if I told him that the look in his eyes ignited my fighting spirit, I would likely be treated as a weirdo.

I staggered, unaccustomed to being on stable ground, and Rigel hurried to prop me up.

"Are you sure you're all right?"

"Yes, I think it's because I don't feel his legs anymore. My own body is confused."

"What—you're saying you already reached a union of soul?!"

Rigel stared at me, in his eyes a mix of exhaustion and awe.

It's not as if I myself have any amazing talents. It's probably all thanks to whatever mysterious being sent me here, but I suppose I don't have to bring that up every single time.

"To ride Veralgon so easily... The hero's power is truly remarkable."

"Captain, isn't he the first since Macuel?"

"Indeed."

Judging by their reactions, this was a particularly challenging dragon. However, it seemed he already had a rider. How unfortunate.

"Hero."

"I know."

"Please use this dragon however you see fit."

Surprised, I said, "Are you sure? Isn't he Mr. Macuel's steed?"

"Macuel is my son's name," said Rigel. "He's already left this world behind."

CHAPTER 4
THE LAY OF THE LAND

THE NEXT DAY, with Rigel leading the way, I flew my dragon to the west. I needed to grow accustomed to riding, and while I was at it, Rigel suggested visiting my territory, which was a half-day's flight from the capital.

Kadann Hill, which was under the direct control of the royal family, had a royal governor that managed its affairs. All I had to do was glance through the occasional documents sent my way and then give the orders for the taxes collected to be sent to the capital. Most of the taxes were paid in goods, but if I requested it, the governor could convert them to coinage.

"Still, you should probably meet the governor and feel out his nature. There are some who would use their lord's absence to fill their pockets with embezzled money," Rigel warned me.

The scenery passing beneath us was repetitive—forest, waste-land, field, the occasional farming village—the same sights over and over. I spotted one city with walls, but that was it. Flying while sharing a dragon's sensations was quite a fresh and invigorating experience, but I grew weary of the landscapes we were navigating. Next time, I decided, I'd fly over the mountains. That would probably be a lot more interesting.

When I looked up, the sun was almost directly above me. Hopefully, we would arrive soon. Through Veralgon's eyes, I could see Rigel waving his hand from the lead. The ability to let my eyes wander while still looking ahead was surprisingly convenient. When I raised my hand to answer his signal, he pointed down and ahead.

Smack-dab in the middle of a flat plain was a bulging hill that looked like an overturned bowl. It was crowned by a circle of monoliths that looked exactly like Stonehenge. This was apparently our destination. Rigel began lowering Greilgon's altitude, and Veralgon followed suit.

The manor for the feudal lord was at the base of the hill. It was far too small to call a castle but too rugged to be a manor. At most, it was a stone structure of ambiguous purpose.

Once we touched down, a man with thinning hair ran out from within. Up close, he turned out to be younger than I thought.

"Hero, dragon rider captain—I have been waiting for you. I am Torson, the governor of this region. Please remember me as Torson, son of Maurson," he said with a deep bow. "The dragon house is that way; please leave your dragon there."

Torson pointed to a sturdy stone structure. Its entrance was a bit too large for a storehouse, but the mountain of miscellaneous items stacked beside it suggested that that was how it was used most of the time. Dragon riders didn't visit that frequently, and I could understand that they'd want to make good use of the space. Rigel had sent an advance party yesterday who had cleaned it out, and those keepers now appeared to take the dragons off our hands. We handed them off and then followed Torson into the manor.

When I looked back, I could see one of the keepers trembling as he led Veralgon along. Veralgon was in a pretty good mood, so there was no need for him to look that terrified. Probably.

The manor was full of orcs. Not living ones, of course. The halls were lined with stuffed orc heads.

"What is all this?"

"It was Sir Aumas, the field marshal before the last, who proposed the interior design. The previous marshal rarely ever came here, so it was left exactly as it was."

So he had been field marshal before Princess Liana, who was my immediate predecessor. While the trip took half a day by dragon, it took quite a while longer to get here by horse. As she usually lived at the capital, Liana had no reason to make the trip. But looking around, I guessed that wasn't the only reason she didn't care for the place.

"Ever since his son was killed, Sir Aumas harbored an intense hatred of orcs. He started displaying the heads of the orcs he'd killed as trophies, and the manor has been left in this sorry state."

I think your real feelings just slipped out there.

"If it isn't to the hero's liking, I can tidy it up."

"Please do."

"I'll arrange for it at once."

He seemed rather happy at the idea. *Well, of course he'd feel down if this is his workspace. I can sympathize.*

We were guided to a spacious central room where we had our meal. Orc heads were on the walls there too, surveying our every move. I saw that even the armrests of the chair he'd pulled out for me were made of bone.

Following my eyes, Torson explained, "Fashioned from the femur of an orc. It was Sir Aumas's idea." *Then those leather curtains are... Let's not think about it.* I would have to tell him to hurry with his cleanup.

When the meal was over, I was to ride around the territory on horseback. It would be easier to get around by dragon, but Torson did not have the talent, and it would be hard to get him on one. Veralgon would threaten him if he approached.

"Horses aren't a problem. The territory isn't that expansive to begin with—we should be back by dinner."

In other words, I would be spending the night here. In a manor littered with dead orcs around every corner. It was not hard to guess what the master bedroom would look like.

"...and apart from our earnings from the harvest, Kadann earns a property tax from two villages and receives offerings from the Hill Temple. We also collect interest on borrowed farm tools and mills, and arbitration and certification fees; there are a multitude of sources..."

An attendant led the horse that Torson sat on as he gave his detailed explanations. His attendant was quite a walker, matching the horse's pace with a composed look on his face. Rigel had stayed behind to look after the dragons, too anxious to leave Veralgon to the keepers.

After a while, we arrived at a small hut. He beckoned me to open the door, upon which, to my astonishment, I found myself face-to-face with a group of naked orcs being struck with whips—this time, they *weren't* stuffed. The living orcs were bound with chains, pushing a thick wooden pillar fastened to smaller horizontal shafts around in a circle.

The hell's this? I occasionally saw that mysterious device in manga and anime but had never in all my worlds seen the real thing. But more to the point, why were there orcs here? Was this also one of that previous lord's hobbies?

"What is all this?" I asked Torson.

"Oi! Ruma!" he called to the man swinging the whip.

The man stopped whipping and turned to us. "Hmm? You need something, Boss?" He looked good-natured, his face quite vacant.

"This is our new field marshal. Pay your respects."

The man knelt before me. "Aye... I mean, I'm in charge of this here mill. The name's Ruma."

"This is a mill?"

"Hmm? Oh, yes. We use the millstone to grind wheat." He pointed to the mysterious device the orcs were turning.

I see, so that's a millstone.

"A portion of the stuff we grind gets sent straight to your pockets—a fee for using the mill. Hee hee hee."

"Hey, now, Ruma. Not in front of the hero."

"Y-yes...uh, no, my apologies." Ruma seemed to curl under Torson's rebuke.

"I apologize for Ruma's discourtesy. He is but an ignorant peasant, so please view him with an open mind."

"I really don't mind. Don't worry."

Torson looked relieved. "You have my gratitude. Ruma might be rough around the edges, but he's kind and earnest. He has never falsified the amount of flour he has produced. It's hard to come by men like him."

"I see."

He did have quite an affable face. Indeed, Ruma wasn't the problem. It was the orcs that bothered me.

"Incidentally, is this orc shed another vestige of my predecessor's predecessor?"

Torson seemed quite perplexed by my question. "No, I believe all mills are roughly the same. I heard they use hairy bulls in the north, but orcs are cheaper and they eat less."

"I see... I imagine a horse would be stronger, though."

"Horses are too expensive. Their maintenance fees are incomparably higher. Perhaps they have some worth in battle, but it's a waste to use them to grind wheat."

Now I was starting to understand. It wasn't just food that the subjugation army snatched up. They abducted orcs to be used as slaves—no more than the cheapest beasts of burden.

As we spoke, one of the orcs suddenly collapsed. Because all of their legs were bound together, the mill's rotation stopped.

"Oi! Who said you could rest?!"

Ruma made his way to the fallen orc and beat him with his whip. After staggering to his feet, the orc clung desperately to its pole to stay upright, but he soon collapsed again.

"Stand!" Ruma screamed, kicking him. This time, the orc didn't try to stand. It curled into a ball on the spot, and Ruma rained lashes down upon its back.

I couldn't watch any more of this. "Hold on, hold on," I said. "Surely, that's enough. Have them all rest for the day. It will die if you keep hitting it like that."

Torson and Ruma looked at me dubiously. "If we give them a break every time an orc gets wobbly, the work's never gonna get done. It'd be a hell of a lot faster to just use him up and buy a new one," Ruma said, sounding much less cordial.

"I'll admit, we shouldn't be treating our protector's assets so roughly," Torson said. "But Ruma does have a point."

Torson evidently shared his opinion. The orcs were being treated as livestock. No, even worse. Dragons and horses were valued more highly and treated far better. It wasn't my place to scold them from an ethical standpoint. What was right in this world was a decision for this world's residents. But given humanity's overwhelming numerical disadvantage, shouldn't there be at least a modicum of consideration of the value of future peace with the orcs?

With that in mind, the scene before my eyes was simply bad business.

On the million-to-one chance that other orcs saw this, peace talks would become impossible. Worst-case scenario, they might fly into a rage and hunt humans to extinction. It wasn't an immediate necessity, but I would need to better their conditions bit by bit. A journey of a thousand miles begins with a single step, as they say. The hut here would be a good starting point.

That said, if I wanted to heed Rigel's warning, this wasn't a topic I could bring up with just anyone. I would need to come up with a different reason for changing how things were done.

"Ahem. Right," I began. "You know how the subjugation forces faced a massive loss?"

"Yes. I've heard rumors, at least," Torson said.

"You can't expect any new gains from orc territory this winter. Meaning, it will be hard to come by any new orcs."

He nodded. "I see. I did hear that the price has been sky-rocketing lately. Perhaps you're right, Hero. Oi, Ruma," he called. "Give them a break."

"Yeah, yeah, if the boss says so." Ruma fetched a key from the wall, then went to the nearest orc and removed the chain binding it to the pillar. Once freed, the orcs formed a line and shambled out of the shed under Ruma's lead. As they left, the one that had fallen shot me a hollow glance and then quickly looked away, following its brethren.

As we were leaving, I asked Torson, "Are there any other orcs in this territory?"

"No, just at the mill. This area isn't so vast, after all."

"I see. Also, can that Ruma fellow speak Orcish?"

Once again, Torson eyed me dubiously. "Orcish?"

"Yes. I mean, I was thinking he could order them around because he understood their language."

"You say some interesting things," Torson answered with a laugh. "The orcs just grunt and snort. They can't speak. They're just like dogs. They can follow simple directions if trained, and that's just about enough to get them to turn grain. There are traveling troupes who have trained orcs to do acrobatics as well."

Again. But what did I expect? I would have to ask around the capital to see if any humans could speak Orcish.

Along the road to our next destination, I caught sight of pitch-black smoke rising from beyond the hills. Something about it was unsettling.

"What is that smoke?" I asked.

Torson stared at the smoke for a moment before answering. "It is coming from the territory of Sir Worgan. A skirmish over succession, I presume. Perhaps a village was set alight?"

"Worgan?" I parroted.

"He rallies all the lords beyond that hill—meaning that he is a great lord uniting the smaller lords. Unfortunately, he died in the last battle. Even worse, his eldest son, who was supposed to succeed him, died of illness, and all that remained were three sons from separate mothers."

That was one of those things that would most definitely be a bother.

"If it disturbs you, shall I conduct a more detailed investigation?"

He apparently thought I had some interest in the succession wars of a neighboring territory. "No, I don't mind, as long as the conflict doesn't cross into Kadann Hill."

I wasn't just neglecting it because it was bothersome, mind you. That was the will of the king.

"Very well. I'm sure they won't lay a hand on the king's land, but I will take the necessary precautions."

"I'm counting on you."

"But there will likely be more bandits after this. They're more troublesome than the lords." Torson sighed.

We arrived at our destination—the first village. It was called West Village. The reason was simple. The territory had two villages; this was the western one. The other village, of course, was called East Village. Apparently, the mill was so far from the villages because it was at the midpoint between the two.

We entered the village to see a line of elderly people in tattered robes awaiting our arrival. Once they caught sight of me, they all prostrated on the spot. I looked to Torson, wondering if that was just how things were done here, but he looked equally confused. *So that is not the norm.* I wondered how I should react as they remained flat on the ground, motionless.

Torson sighed and stepped out. "What are you people doing?"

"Oh! It's you, Governor," one answered without raising their head. "I take it that the esteemed personage you have with you is the new lord."

"That he is. He's been appointed as the newest protector of Kadann Hill—a hero from another world who has taken his place as field marshal to lead the armies in His Majesty's place. Hero, this is Warren, the mediator of West Village. Please remember him."

"To be graced with a visit from such a noble figure is the greatest honor of every villager. However, we could hardly look the hero in his divine eyes, and thus must remain on the lowly ground."

"Seriously, what happened?"

"Yesterday, a messenger from the governor came, suggesting we prepare something to celebrate the hero who has become our new lord."

"Indeed, I sent the message. Then why not present a cask of wine, as is custom?"

"Unfortunately, this year's crop failed. It was so poor, I was about to plead to lower the land tax. Next, I heard that the hero was a fearsome fighter who slaughtered an entire army of orcs on his own. How could I, in the same breath, offer such a hero our loyalty and congratulations, then beg him to lower our taxes? The thought frightened me, terrified me... Everyone in the village conferred, and the oldest of us got together to make our plea. Please, please...honor these old bones, and at least let the rest of the villagers live."

After prattling on, the village chief skillfully presented his neck, remaining prostrate. *My story is certainly getting blown out of proportion again.*

Torson looked at me. "Hero, what shall we do?"

That's what I wanted to ask.

"Mr. Torson, how was the harvest?" I said.

"It's certainly less than last year's. We will make it through the winter, but only with some days of hunger. It will be a harsh year, especially for the youngest and the old. A few will die. That much is certain. Worst-case scenario, the remaining townsfolk might take flight. That will mean less labor available from now on. I believe the tax reduction is valid."

"In that case—"

"However, the increase in the price of food will also raise the value of produce. If we take the same amount of crops in taxes as last year, they will be worth far more in monetary value. Just for reference."

Torson's expression was unchanging, but his eyes were prying. Perhaps in his own way, he was trying to see what sort of person his new superior was.

"At the moment, am I right in saying we have enough income to cover our expenses?"

"Yes, milord. We will get through it by the skin of our teeth, but we will make it."

"Then I will permit the reduction. You can work out the details."

"I'm sure the people will be relieved and grateful when they hear of your generosity." Torson lowered his head, then turned back to the elderly folks and declared, "The hero has graciously accepted your plea to lower property tax!"

There were immediate cheers.

"Now, Warren, the hero wishes to see his own territory. Show him around town."

"But of course! Hero, come with me."

"Don't take too much time. The hero still has to see East Village and the Hill Temple."

"Very well, I'll be brief. It's not a large village, in any case."

As I listened in on their exchange, something suddenly occurred to me. "Oh, right, East Village isn't too far, is it?"

"That's correct."

"Then could you send a messenger while I'm looking around?"

"What shall I tell them?"

"They'll need a reduction too, won't they?"

Torson immediately understood what I meant. "You're right. We wouldn't want to be welcomed like this again. I'll tell them in advance. Oi, Rick!" he called to his attendant, who had melted into the background.

"Yes!"

"I need you to pass a message to East Village. Could you be quick about it?"

"Leave it to me!"

Before he had even finished speaking, Rick was racing off at an incredible pace.

"Hey! Wait! Rick! Get back here!" Torson hurried after him. "I haven't told you the message yet! Good grief, what an impatient one you are."

Torson relayed the message in full, and once he had heard it, the attendant took off mumbling something under his breath.

He apparently had to keep repeating it or he would forget it. It reminded me a bit of rakugo, that oft-humorous storytelling art from my original world.

Now Torson turned back to the elderly folk.

"Oh, and Warren. Do something about those pilgrim clothes already."

"You're right."

The group quickly began stripping off their tattered robes. The clothes underneath, while old and worn, were all clean and well kept. I later learned that those robes were the proper uniform for making a petition to their lord.

As I'd expected, I arrived at East Village to find the impatient attendant had made matters worse. I was as much a demon as a hero to them—a legendary figure who had devastated an entire orcish legion single-handedly—and the village chief shuddered upon receiving a completely incomprehensible message from such an individual. Every single villager was dressed in the pilgrim clothes and waiting for us. While I managed to clear up the misunderstanding quickly enough, the advance message had been completely pointless.

❂

Our last stop was the temple that carried out all the religious rites of the region. It was a rather small place that stood at the foot of Kadann Hill.

"When the head priest placed the sacred diadem atop His Majesty's head in the divine name of God above, I was the one who brought the diadem to him."

A small rat-faced priest who proclaimed himself to be the master of the temple pointed at a mural and smiled proudly. The painting depicted an old man in a white robe placing a diadem across upon the head of a small child. While the child shared characteristics with the boy king I knew, he was even younger.

According to the master, the temple was a small one, with only three priests permanently stationed, but it had a high status as the site of the coronation ceremony.

"Every single head priest the country has ever had, without exception, once served as a master of the Hill Temple," the priest said. "Do you understand what that means, Hero?"

His ingratiating smile and fluttering lashes were a clear attempt to curry favor. What a shrewd man he was, to intimidate me with the mantle of borrowed authority and suck up at the same time.

"This temple does not derive its authority from the king. When the truly faithful offer their prayers in our halls, they are immediately gifted by the grace of God. A blind man opened his eyes through prayer. A child born lame not only stood upright, but he even had his leg straightened."

For quite some time now, the master's mouth had not stopped moving for even a moment. He was really putting it to good use. Perhaps having grown weary of the ceaseless boasts, Torson finally interrupted.

"Then if I pray, will the youth return to my hair?"

"Certainly." The master's expression turned sullen. "God works his miracles for everyone. Only if you are truly faithful, though."

It was dawning on me that these two didn't get along.

The master turned to me. "No matter what the impious say, there are no doubts that God's grace dwells in this temple. Otherwise, why would so many visit each day, seeking salvation? We have pilgrims forming long lines on a regular basis."

"If you're that prosperous, perhaps I should expect some sizable offerings this year. I've heard that worshipping here isn't cheap." Torson grinned, clearly feeling he'd beaten the fellow at his own game. In this world, the priests were a source of income for the land's protector—most often the feudal lord.

"Urk... Oh well, there have been so many skirmishes breaking out these days that we're getting fewer and fewer visitors. Certainly, when you boil it down, I am no more than a servant of God. I couldn't possibly take money from the poor folk facing such hardships as it is."

"A shame."

Torson said no more. Watching the master scrambling for a response, he seemed satisfied.

"Is the situation that bad in these parts?" I said.

The master, who had been glaring at Torson, looked quite relieved at the change in topic.

"Yes, you don't know the half of it. Many lords lost their lives in the last battle. Battles for inheritance are breaking out all over the place. In these parts, the leaders who united northern Morsharz and southern Kerulgarz never returned. In Morsharz, the lord's younger brother has propped up his late brother's infant son as a candidate and settled the dispute. The south has not gone so easily. After Worgan—oh, he's the late lord of Kerulgarz—after he fell in battle, his eldest son followed soon after. He had three other sons. But the troubling thing is, he had sown his seed in three different fields. Luckily, the eldest son had no children, or it would become even more complicated. Each house is vying to be the rightful successor. What a tragedy! Siblings who share blood, led about by treacherous retainers and forced to cut down their kin!"

The master peeked at my face before going on.

"Kerulgarz's lesser lords have split into three factions and are burning down one another's territories. Many have had their homes burnt to the ground. Such pitiful folk. They have no houses to stave off the cold, nor any food to keep them going. They've lost even the seeds for next year. I'm sure many lives will be lost this winter. How truly terrifying. How deplorable. It is hell on earth. The lords burning down territories hope to regain their losses by stealing from the other factions. At this rate, even more villages will be burned. The innocent will find themselves on the streets—a portion will turn to banditry and bring about even more tragedy. I heard you reduced your taxes to save the starving people of this territory. What a noble deed! That some- one so filled with benevolence graced these lands must have been God's pity on the powerless! Might you consider wielding that power for the sake of the people of Kerulgarz?"

After saying all of that in one breath, he stared at me intently with pleading eyes. Sure, he sounded righteous, but it was all a bit fishy. How did he already know what happened at the other villages? How did he find all that out so quickly?

He looked as seedy as a rat, and rats could be treacherous. And yet, he might be a candidate to be the next head priest. I needed to be careful. I suspected I would be in for a load of trouble if I let him lead me around.

"Master, I'm sorry to say, I have not been in this world for long, and I do not know their circumstances. If I stick my nose into this business without enough information, I might make the situation even worse."

The master rubbed my hand and brought his face close to mine.

"Then I shall teach you. Of course, it is completely up to your discretion which side you choose to support, but I'm sure I can help you make that decision. First, the oldest one was born to a lowly bloodline, and he is known as a terribly rude man. On this occasion, word has it that he led his troops with a torch in one hand and personally set fire to every village in his path. On top of that, I have heard he captured the female farmworkers smoked out by the flames and made them his playthings. He is strong in battle but lacking in intelligence, without a shred of faith in God. If his funds ran low, he would go as far as to ransack a temple. These are all only rumors, but I've overheard whispers that he was the one who offered poison to the older brother. I must call him a completely immoral individual.

"On to the youngest son. He is only six years of age, and I do not see how he could unite the warriors to face the enemies of God. It seems he himself does not wish to fight against his brothers, but his grandfather on his mother's side has ambitions. He intends to use the opportunity to make a puppet of the infant and install himself as the one in power. It's clear what will happen if such a greedy man seizes control. The other lords won't stay quiet."

The master finally took a breath. I was amazed he didn't pass out after prattling on for that long.

"Finally, we have the middle son. He had originally been sent to the monastery, where he pledged his service to God. He is smart and virtuous. He thoroughly understands God's teachings and has upheld them all his life. He left the monastery for the funeral of his father and dear eldest, and once he returned to his hometown, he was met with one brother wielding violence against the people, the other surrounded by disloyal retainers with no voice of his own. At that moment, he received a revelation from God. Someone must set this right! He knew it was his mission! Without joining forces with either side, he gathered only those whose hearts were pure and took action."

His allegiances were obvious.

"You're pretty knowledgeable about this whole situation," I said, keeping my doubt out of my tone.

"If you know not the world's toils, then what would you pray for? Be that as it may, Hero, the weak are suffering even as we stand. I leave it up to you who you side with, but please lend your power to stop the fighting."

After so blatantly praising the middle son, he had quite a bit of nerve to claim he was leaving it to me. *No doubt he has good ears, but I don't know how much I can trust what comes out of his mouth.*

I didn't intend to get involved, no matter what he told me. That was my promise to the king.

"In this matter, I believe the first step would be to seek the king's arbitration," I said. "If, after that, anyone is so impudent as to go against his will, then I will wield my power in His Majesty's name."

At the mention of the king, an unpleasant look spread over the master's face. "Ah, well... The lords do not like it when the king gets involved in their domestic affairs."

"Then my intervention should be even less welcome. It looks like I have no business here."

"B-but—"

Torson interjected, "Marshal, sir. We're running late."

"You're right, I nearly forgot. Apologies, Master, but I must take my leave."

I wasn't supposed to have anything scheduled after this, but I'd had it with his endless monologues. I quickly stood and put the temple behind me.

CHAPTER 5

THE PRINCESS OF MORSHARZ

"THANKS, TORSON. You saved me back there."

"No, I was growing sick and tired of it too," he replied with a wry smile. He was probably a good man, deep down. I got the feeling I'd be able to get along with him just fine.

"Will we be back by sunset?" I asked. The master's idle chatter wasted much of the day away.

"Yes, we should get there in ten minutes. We'll be right in time for dinner."

Glancing south, I saw a smoke rising from a different location than before. The master's character assessment aside, I knew for certain that something foul was going on beyond those hills. It hurt my heart to allow it to continue, but surely battles between humans were supposed to be solved by humans.

"Eeeek!" I heard a young woman scream.

Following the sound, I caught sight of a figure approaching. She was dressed in pilgrim's clothes and clutched a child to her chest. Two horsemen were chasing her.

What perfect timing.

I wasn't going to aggressively interfere with human strife in this world, but I was not callous enough to ignore a woman pleading for help before my very eyes. *A good rampage now and again would be a nice change of pace—why not feel like a hero for once?*

First, I observed the horsemen kicking up dust in the distance. They were fully armed. They couldn't be bandits—their equipment was of too high quality. Perhaps they had something to do with the wars raging next door. *I wouldn't want any trouble...*

Manifesting a spear of light in my right hand, I checked with Torson. "Am I right in assuming that disorder within the territory comes under its protector's jurisdiction?"

"Yes, certainly. The lord has the right and obligation to deal with anyone who inflicts harm upon his people, no matter who they may be."

That made the decision simple. I turned toward them and spurred my horse, prompting it to rear up. The action had no meaning—I just thought it would look heroic. As a matter of fact, I could have simply tossed my spear without asking any questions, but then the whole thing would have been over in an instant, and what would be the point of that?

"You must be pretty shameless to gang up on a woman with a child!" I called out. "From your outfits, I take it you're no ordinary bandits! Identify yourselves!"

In the time it took for me to make my declaration, the woman ran up to me and was now clinging onto my horse. *Erk, that makes it hard to move.*

"Hero! Please save me!" She looked up at me and removed the hood of her pilgrim's robe, allowing two tidy bundles of blonde hair to spill out.

Surprisingly, the face that had emerged belonged to a young girl of perhaps fifteen or sixteen. Since she was holding a child, I'd expected her to be older. She didn't have any outstanding traits that caught the eye, but on closer inspection, her features carried a sort of rustic charm. When she looked at me with upturned eyes, she stimulated my primordial urge to protect, all of a sudden filling me with motivation.

I was ready now, and I turned back to see how the enemy would react.

Taking me by complete surprise, they had dismounted their horses and removed their helmets. *There's no way I can attack them now!* I felt as if someone had dangled a treat before me and then snatched it away.

As I watched in a daze, they drew their horses up to me and bowed their heads. Torson tugged on my sleeve and whispered, "They are offering their gratitude, Hero."

Torson had also dismounted by the time I looked at him. I hurriedly erased my spear, got off my horse, and reciprocated the bow.

"I take it you are the hero from another world. We charged into your esteemed territory while fully armed, disrupting your peace for our own selfish reasons—and for that, you have my humblest apologies. I am a knight in service to Great Lord Gordan of Morsharz, and my name is Chrost." As I recalled, a great lord was a lord who presided over an entire region rather than a territory.

"I serve Gordan as well. I go by Ekmas."

Introductions finished, the knights lowered their heads again.

"I see," I said. "How courteous of you."

Their attitude came so out of left field, I wasn't sure how to react. *Wait. Morsharz? They came from the north rather than the south?*

"I am Governor Torson of Kadann Hill. You mentioned your reasons. Would you care to elaborate?" Torson asked in my stead.

"I cannot give details on the internal affairs of the house, but we came chasing someone who fled from the territory. Could you please return the child and woman to us?"

The girl hiding behind me anxiously pressed up against me. *Oh, she's quite big for being so small. That is and will be my only comment on the matter.*

I wasn't the sort to hand over a cowering maiden just because I was asked to.

"I decline."

Of course, they didn't automatically back down. Their courteous attitude did not crumble, however, and they simply repeated their request.

"In the case that a fugitive from another territory is found, the law states that they must be turned over to their original lord. Please hand her over."

Hmm, so there's a law for that. How troubling. It was my policy to respect local laws wherever I could. Even I couldn't just cut down two fine gentlemen who lowered their heads and sought out a peaceful resolution. But wasn't there anything I could do? The sensation on my back felt like a plea to save a feeble maiden. Was there even the slightest pretext that I could use as a shield?

Sensing my intentions, Torson came to my aid yet again.

"By her clothing, she must be a pilgrim to the Hill Temple. Safeguarding pilgrims is the duty of the lord who oversees the temple."

Nice work, Torson! Now I had a justification on my side. If that wasn't enough, then it would be a matter of strength. I would just beat them up—not lethally, of course—and send them packing. *Right, no killing. If anyone died, then that would be cause for the rest of their soldiers to come after me.* As long as no one died, we might be able to find common ground. That was generally how it worked in all worlds. If it were simply a matter of a farm girl on the run, it could likely be solved with money, although it might prove to be a problem if she were the lord's favorite or something. *Come to think of it, he did say there were house affairs involved.*

I readied myself to use force if necessary, although the weight on my back constrained me.

"If she is a pilgrim, she should be carrying a pilgrim charm," Chrost replied. "If she is not a pilgrim, you come under no duty to protect her."

Torson's argument was defeated in the blink of an eye. Just to be sure, I turned and looked her in the eye, but she shook her head. She didn't have a pilgrim charm.

"I make my plea once again. I swear it on my sword that nothing ill will befall her. Please hand her to us." The knight named Chrost took a step forward.

"Hero! Please save me!" the girl pleaded. "I'll serve you however I can! Please, proclaim that you place me under your protection!"

I had no idea what would happen if I made that proclamation. I gave Torson a quizzical look. He nodded in response, but his eyes told me that this was going to be a pain. Such a proclamation would likely be a point of no return. Perhaps I would have to provide for her for the rest of my life.

But, whatever. I had the resources to support one girl, and I'd taken it this far. The train had already left the station. Why not ride it to the end?

"This girl has been placed under my protection," I declared. "If you insist on taking her back, you will have to defeat me first!"

"The field marshal has guaranteed her every right. Anyone who infringes upon those rights will be deemed an enemy." Torson's words bolstered my proclamation, but his expression screamed, *Oh, now you've gone and done it.*

"Then there is nothing we can do. For the time being, we entrust her to you. However, we must return and report this to our lord."

With that courteous farewell, the two knights retreated ever so anticlimactically.

"I am Megriel, daughter of Cardon, the former great lord of Morsharz. My friends call me Meg. This is my brother, Odon, the current great lord of Morsharz."

She was higher ranked than I had anticipated. When I peeked at Torson, he shrugged as if to say, *What did I tell you?*

"Mr. Torson, did you know who she was?"

"If I did, I would have told you."

What was I supposed to do now? I'd shoved my head straight into trouble. This wasn't how it was supposed to turn out.

"Mr. Torson, do you think we could call those knights back?"

"Well, a vow of protection and servitude, meaning a vow of vassalage, is one of the weightiest vows one can make."

It's that serious? I don't remember hearing anything about vassalage.

"I said I would protect her, not make her my vas—"

"But I said I would serve you," Megriel interrupted. "And you claimed you would protect me."

She looked up at me pleadingly.

"I did say that, but... Torson, was that really enough to establish it? Shouldn't such an important vow be a bit more... you know, formal? Shouldn't there be some proper oaths or a ceremony?"

"There is no formal procedure. As long as both sides proclaim protection and service before three or more of those without falsehood, the vow officially goes into effect."

"What do you mean by 'those without falsehood'?"

"Those whose testimony cannot be placed under scrutiny in trial. Namely, those in service to God, those who rule over land, those in the grips of death, a maiden speaking about her own purity, a pregnant woman speaking about the father of her child, and a knight discussing noble vows. The words of these people are to be accepted as the truth as long as no evidence points to the contrary. I have been knighted, for what it's worth, so the conditions have been fulfilled. That is precisely why they obediently withdrew."

I see. Still, while the law seemed to put those in power at an advantage, it also had some unusual considerations for women. Interesting.

"In that case, what if you just deny it?"

My words seemed to displease him greatly. "We are those without falsehood precisely because we can never misrepresent the truth. I will never lie about a vow."

It was clear that he would hold firm. He really was a serious and sincere man, as was to be expected of the governor of the region.

"What's more, those knights are going to report the matter to their lord, which complicates the situation," he continued. "If it becomes known that you abandoned your vows, your credibility will be damaged—as well as the credibility of His Majesty who appointed you."

Yes, that would be bad. But which would be worse: getting the king involved or finding myself in the middle of a territorial dispute? I was definitely going to need more information.

I turned to the girl. "This is no place to talk. Let's return to the manor for the time being. I can hear your story there. Can you ride a horse? Here, you can ride mine."

Her face lit up. *Whatever else, she has the sort of smile that makes me want to protect her.*

As we approached, Veralgon came out to greet us. It was apparently time for the dragons to be fed.

Odon, Great Lord of Morsharz, froze stiff before the massive white beast.

"Hero! You're finally back!"

Rigel jogged up. He had been supervising the keepers in their work. When he noticed the woman beside me, his eyes widened. "Why, if it isn't Lady Megriel! You've grown up beautifully!" Rigel got down on one knee.

"It's been a while. I'm happy to see you haven't changed one bit, Rigel." Megriel lifted the hem of her pilgrim clothes ever so slightly to curtsy.

I looked at Rigel. "You two know each other?"

"Yes. Do you remember how I said I used to look after the princess? At the time, Megriel was her attendant."

"Not exactly an attendant," she said. "I was essentially responsible for playing with her."

I see. Small world we live in.

"Veralgon is as beautiful as ever." Megriel approached the dragon without a hint of fear. She acted so naturally that I almost failed to react.

"Wait! Stop!" I cried.

She was reaching out to touch Veralgon's pure-white plumage. I manifested a spear of light out of reflex, but I knew I wouldn't make it in time. And yet, what I feared never happened.

"It's all right, Hero," she said, smiling. "We've met before."

She stroked Veralgon without a care in the world. Even the most seasoned of keepers struggled with him. His eyes reflected mild perturbation, but he meekly submitted to her touch.

It seemed Megriel had the talent.

"It's a real shame," Rigel muttered.

"What is?"

"Megriel. If she had been born a man, she could have become a first-rate dragon rider. The nation's champion, even."

I heard a wail, nearly a scream. I turned to see that Odon was bawling his eyes out. Torson was frantically trying to soothe him, but the floodgates showed no signs of closing.

◦|ﾒ|◦

After young Odon was tucked into bed, we gathered to hear Megriel's story. She flinched as she entered the parlor, which was the room with the most orc...*things* of all. She looked at me with a mix of fear and amazement. The implied accusation in her gaze was unfair—I was not responsible for this collection. *To tell the truth, I was beginning to feel that that previous field marshal's hatred of orcs had gone so far that it looped back around into love.*

"Now let's hear what you have to say," I said, offering a chair made of orc bone.

With some hesitation, she took a seat, then began to tell her story.

"My uncle was always kind to me, and he doted on me and Odon. So I felt at ease when he said he would act as the protector until Odon came of age. Yet once the position was his, he became someone else entirely. He was sitting in the lord's seat by the end of the day, acting as if he himself were lord. My brother and I were confined to a room in the tower. Those who protested were severely punished. One day, it was decided that we were to be moved from Morsharz castle to my uncle's manor. Publicly, it was said that the move was meant to help Odon's feeble body recuperate. Still, even if Odon was lord in name alone, it would be unusual to remove him from his rightful castle. We suspected something was amiss, and before long, someone who still had a conscience secretly informed us that our uncle intended to kill us. If we were in his own territory, he could easily have us served something poisonous and conceal the real cause of death."

She stopped for a moment, trembling timidly, then continued.

"On the day of our move, I saw my chance and we fled. It had been arranged for us to depend on a lesser lord who opposed my uncle's rule, but my pursuers got the better of me, and I never made it there. I had no choice but to flee to these lands, where I hoped to receive protection from the temple, but we were spotted before we reached it... The rest is as you know."

What a horrible uncle. However, this kind of story was common in every world. I could understand how the people supporting her uncle felt. Humanity had suffered a crushing defeat, while civil wars were breaking out all over. The curtain was opening on a harsh era. In such difficult times, who would look up to an infant as their lord? What they needed now was a strong, dependable ruler. On top of that, it seemed that this world's law was relatively vague when it came to inheritance, with none of the regulations spelling anything out clearly. That was also pretty common.

"So, Megriel," I said. "What do you want from me?"

"I want justice. I want you to lend a hand, to return power to its rightful owner."

"Meaning that you want me to steal the seat of the great lord back from your uncle."

"Yes." Megriel nodded. There was a profound resolve in her eyes. I sighed at the sight of her unwavering expression.

"Why not give up on that seat and be satisfied with your new-found safety?"

Her expression stiffened. Torson's thoroughly fed-up stare was so intense that I could feel it without even turning around. Rigel didn't show any reaction. The old man knew what His Majesty wanted from me.

"The position of great lord was passed to us from our father," she said. "He got it from his father. It is our duty to pass the honor down to the next generation! I shall not let it fall to the hands of a usurper! Please, oh, please, won't you lend me your aid?"

The girl who had stroked the white dragon and smiled was nowhere to be seen. The one standing before me now, pleading desperately, was a noble lady willing to give up anything to do her duty. I could see a hint of the boy king in her.

A girl of such tender age burdened with such heavy responsibility—what ordinary man could simply refuse her pleas for help?

"I understand your resolve."

Her expression loosened ever so slightly at those words.

"But I'll ask you one more time. Couldn't you leave Morsharz to your uncle? If you agree to those terms, I'll do everything in my power to guarantee your safety."

Yep, you heard me! I'm the hero! I do what other men cannot! Sorry, but between this girl and His Majesty, the burdens they bear are on completely different levels. I can't treat them equally.

"Why..." Her expression turned to despair. Torson, who had kept his silence the whole time, took a step forward, unable to bear it any longer.

"Hero, the protection of a vassalage vow is not simply bodily protection. It includes the protection of the vassal's rights as well."

What? You're making it sound like this is my fault.

"Sir Torson, this is the hero's decision to make," Rigel chided him.

Torson's mouth opened again, but under the pressure of Rigel's intense gaze, it closed without a word. He bowed a quick apology and stepped back.

An awkward silence followed. It seemed I would need to explain my thought process.

"To be honest, from my position as field marshal, it doesn't matter who rules Morsharz as long as they swear their loyalty to the king." I paused to gauge Megriel's reaction. Her head was still hanging and she said nothing, so I went on. "My greatest fear is that the succession battle in Morsharz worsens and drags the lesser lords into the mix. You're aware of what is happening in Kerulgarz, aren't you?"

Currently, the lesser lords south of Kadann Hill were wrapped up in an intense civil war for the seat of great lord. Villages were burned, farmers were killed, and the survivors were tormented by starvation or taken as slaves. It seemed clear that the same thing was about to happen in Morsharz.

I continued. "Humanity lost many knights in the last battle. We must avoid wasting any more troops in civil war. With that in mind, the optimal solution would be for me to hand you over to your uncle, even if my reputation is thrown in the gutter as a result." I could hear Torson swallow his breath. "Of course, I understand the weight of a vow. That's why, instead, I propose this: Give up on Morsharz. You trade your inheritance for your safety. Gordan gives up on murdering you, gaining legitimacy instead. I, meanwhile, will lose half of my reputation and will have to take charge of you. But I retain the other half, and I gain Morsharz's loyalty. I don't think we'll get a better deal."

Megriel raised her face, determination in her eyes. She refused to give up.

"Hero. Is it possible to carry out a transaction in good faith with a man who took advantage of his nephew's youth to usurp a seat?" she asked. "Rigel, I'm sure you remember my late father's devotion to the throne. He galloped out with the famed Knights of Morsharz the moment he received the princess's summons."

"Indeed. Cardon's loyalty has been burned deep into my mind. He was a good knight and friend." Rigel nodded, looking into the distance, his expression still stern.

"On the other hand, my uncle had won a number of lesser lords to his side, using minor losses as an excuse to exempt him and many others from military service. For that reason, these past few years, my father was forced to lead free knights and mercenaries rather than skilled warriors on the battlefield. Thinking back on it now, perhaps that was all a ploy to get my father killed. If my father had command of all his elites during the war, perhaps the princess—"

Rigel twitched. The scales had tilted in his head.

"We've gotten off track. My point is: Can you expect the same loyalty from that insincere man as you could from my father?" She stood from her seat, then walked in front of me and got down on one knee. "I renew my vows to serve the king and the hero just as faithfully—no, even more faithfully than my father. If you leave Morsharz to us, all fifteen hundred of Morsharz's horsemen will sally forth whenever and wherever the hero commands it. Among them, the three hundred of my father's retinue are capable of night operations and ambushes. They will definitely be of use to you."

She pledged, not to the king or the marshal, but to the hero. Splendid. Whether her plea was feasible, she had highlighted what I stood to gain. She was a fast thinker. However, her proposal lacked the most important feature.

"Sure, if I help you, we'll have an advantage in battle," I said. "But ultimately, battle will become unavoidable. How many of those fifteen hundred will be left when it's all over? Is it possible to keep them unharmed?"

"Of course. I have an idea." She remained on her knees, but her gaze was resolute.

"An idea?"

"Yes. Truth be told, only a select few of the lesser lords actively support my uncle. Most of them are sitting back and waiting for the matter to be resolved."

That sounds pretty plausible.

"If we can get them on our side, we can ensure our numbers. Then, if we take out the others, who have voiced their support for my uncle, it will be over in no time at all. I presume there will be barely any bloodshed."

Was that supposed to be a plan? It sounded barely thought-out. I had no confidence in it at all.

"Aren't you being a little too optimistic?"

"It's all right," she declared with a fearless smile. "Even if I can't do it alone, it is possible with the might of the hero."

I don't really get it, but she seems incredibly confident.

"You won't even need to swing your sword," she continued. "If I have the hero's support, then the ones who are on the fence will come over to my side. If the plan doesn't work out, then present me to my uncle and ask for peace. I'll accept it."

My reputation takes a tumble in that scenario! But I had to admit that she had commendable resolve. And if all I had to do was lend her my name, then I wouldn't have to spill blood, I wouldn't have to damage my reputation, and I'd get an army to boot. It was certainly an appealing proposal.

Worst-case scenario, I could attack the uncle's army with Veralgon. In that case, I'd spill some blood and earn some grudges. The king would not be pleased, but the situation would be put in order.

I sought Rigel's opinion. He silently nodded when our eyes met.

"Very well," I said. "If you're that sure, I'll stand behind you."

Megriel's face lit up like a torch. *That innocent, carefree smile... I feel like I understand her less and less all the time.*

†|ö|†

Looking down, I saw Morsharz Castle at the top of a hill, a sturdy, square, stone structure with a tower at each corner. I breathed a sigh of relief. To the west, I saw the sun's final moments. In a moment, the earth that had been so bright was dyed the deep blue of night.

I had barely made it before sundown. In a world without streetlamps, night meant true darkness. Night flying was beyond me—I would hardly be able to tell up from down with just the light of the stars.

I was considering where to land when Megriel, her arms wrapped around my waist, tugged on my clothes and brought her lips to my ear.

"The dragon! In the castle! Yard! Think you can?!" The wind was so noisy that she had to scream.

The walled courtyard was spacious enough. It would probably work out. I nodded to her and sent the signal to Rigel behind me, and then we slowly spiraled toward the earth.

⋮|✗|⋮

When I'd decided to go along with her plan, Megriel had said, "Even the opportunistic lords can't change their allegiances so easily once they've already declared their positions. We will need to make your existence known and bring them over to our side while they're still sitting on the fence."

With everyone in agreement, we had immediately set to work.

"I think we need to head to the castle before dusk," she'd said. "My uncle is away with his troops searching for me. Most of those remaining should be supportive of our cause. If we arrive with the hero before he returns, we will be able to take the castle."

Thus, we'd set off for Morsharz Castle without pausing for dinner. Once we captured this symbol of the great lords' authority, with my—or rather, the king's appointed field marshal's—backing, they could assert their own legitimacy.

⋮|✗|⋮

As we descended, I could see people moving about the castle grounds in a frenzy. The four towers had anti-dragon weaponry on top, but the castle garrison was nowhere to be seen. With no one to shoot at us, we were safe. Once we had reached an appropriate altitude, I had Veralgon roar to send a signal to the castle.

When we touched down, the flapping of the dragon's mighty wings sent sand and dust flying. This never happened at the grand dragon house, which grew grass to prevent it. Coughing up a storm, I helped Megriel dismount. She had already discarded her pilgrim's clothes for women's riding gear that had been left behind by Liana, the previous field marshal.

Once the dust had settled, a well-built middle-aged man rushed into the yard.

He spoke in a raspy voice between gasps. "D-dragon rider... I am Jura, retainer to Great Lord Odon of Morsharz. What business have you—" Suddenly, he noticed the girl standing behind me. "Megriel! Are you unharmed?! I was so worried about you!"

"Yes, I'm fine. No need to worry. Where is my uncle?"

"Gordan has led the retinue out in search of you. He should be home soon. Incidentally, where might Odon be?"

"Odon has been taken under the protection of Kadann Hill," she replied.

Odon hadn't a sliver of talent and couldn't ride dragons, so we'd left him behind in the orc-bedecked manor.

"Kadann Hill? Then that gentleman is..."

"He is the hero. Jura, hurry and close the gate. How much of the garrison remains?"

"Hrm? Around fifty, milady. But why close the gate?"

"Fifty? That should be enough. Have them take their stations."

"B-but..."

"Did you not hear me? Station the garrison and close the gate. Don't open it when my uncle returns."

"Y-yes! At once!"

It was clear she wouldn't take no for an answer, so, as hesitant as he was, the retainer complied. Her undaunted attitude really made her seem like the daughter of a famed house.

Once the retainer was out of sight, she began walking toward the castle. "Well then, Hero, there's no need to wait around here. Follow me."

"Leave Veralgon to me," Rigel called out as he helped the keepers who had ridden with him dismount. I offered him a subtle bow and then followed Megriel.

Megriel led me to the roof of the main compound. From its position at the top of the hill, it was probably possible to see a great distance in the daytime. But now that the sun had set, I could only make out faint silhouettes of the highs and lows of the terrain.

Nevertheless, Megriel leaned out, searching for something.

"Look over there!"

She suddenly pointed to the east. Squinting into the distance, I could see the flicker of many torches. They were moving at a rapid pace.

"That's..."

"My uncle and his retinue."

So there they were. They somehow managed to maintain their formation perfectly while riding in the dark—at that speed, no less. She wasn't lying when she said they could work at night. They were already on her uncle's side. If possible, I wanted to obtain them in one piece. I could only hope they'd give up without a fight.

Megriel continued to stare at the lines of lights for a while. Then, apparently deciding they were close enough, she smiled faintly. "All right, let's go to the parlor."

She started back down and I scurried after her. We loitered around the parlor till the retainer rushed in.

"Megriel! Gordan has arrived with the retinue. He is demanding to be let in."

"Very well. Then we'll have to start by talking to my uncle. Open the gate."

What a peculiar order. If she was going to open the gate that easily, what did she close it for?

"Are you sure?" I asked after the retainer rushed off.

"Yes, I don't mind. We're here anyway, so I thought we might have a nice chat. He won't do anything extreme as long as you and Veralgon are with me."

Perhaps she had a point. It was best to solve things through negotiation.

"Then you could have left the gate open."

"I need to make it clear whom the castle belongs to. More importantly, Hero, won't you lend me your sword?"

"This one?"

"Yes. I feel rather helpless unarmed."

Something about this was unsettling to me, but I figured I could always fight with my spears of light if it came to it. I pulled my sword from its scabbard and held it out, but she stopped me.

"Err, if possible, I want the sword belt in its entirety."

Oops, right. This was supposed to be a discussion. Not really appropriate to show up with swords drawn.

I had to fiddle with the buckle for a bit—the fasteners of this world boasted quite a convoluted design. After opening it somehow, I passed the belt to her, and she skillfully equipped and adjusted it.

"So. How do I look?" She spun around with a mischievous smile. She didn't look half-bad.

Veralgon's roar echoed out, and I could hear the neighs of spooked horses and sounds of a boisterous crew gathering in the yard.

"He's here." With a satisfied smile, she took her place beside an ornamented chair that was most likely reserved for the head of the house. She was an imposing sight to behold as she stood at attention, almost like a full-fledged knight.

"Come here, Hero," she said, motioning for me to stand on the other side of the chair. I had no reason not to. *Ever since we arrived, she's been acting like a completely different person.*

The ruckus was already dying down—meaning the horses and their riders were well trained. *Impressive.* Before long, the door to the parlor opened and three men entered, led by the retainer.

The square-faced man in the center with the short hair and beard was probably her uncle. The other two who walked one step behind him were his guards.

All three had swords at their hips but carried no other weapons. They hadn't come to fight.

The uncle started off by coming up to me and bowing.

"I am Gordan, son of Maldon, who was the head of Morsharz two generations ago. I currently serve as the lord of Conharz. I take it you are the field marshal who commands the king's armies, the hero summoned from another world."

"How courteous... Ahem, yes. I am the hero."

I was taken aback by his attitude. This was the villain who'd plotted to kill his niece and nephew so he could seize the territory? I had readied myself to face an outrageously fiendish man; this wasn't at all what I'd expected. In contrast to the image I'd created in my mind, the man who stood before me seemed honest and sincere. Middle-aged with specks of white in his hair, he wasn't that old, but the deep-set wrinkles in his face spoke of the troubles he had faced in life.

"You safely delivered my nephew to me, and for that, I am in your debt." His head was lowered and his voice ached with fatigue. Then his mood changed as he turned to Megriel. "Meg! What is the meaning of all this?! What nonsense did you get up to this time?!"

I want to know that too.

"Nothing much," she said. "I just took a short trip to enlist the hero's assistance."

"Assistance? I can't think of anything we would need his help for!"

"Sure you can. What about the succession?"

"We already discussed that! For the time being, I will act as the land's protector, but I'll leave all management to you. Same as we've always done things. What more do you want?!"

That's a little different from what I heard. I had a vague idea of what was going on.

"What do I want? Plenty!" Megriel spat. "That arrangement gives you all the military authority! I want to lead an army and fight like my father."

"I know. You have what it takes to be a general. I'm sure the retinue would gladly follow your lead. But the same can't be said for the lesser lords. As long as you're a woman, there's little we can do about it! I thought we already reached an agreement."

"That's old news. Things have changed. I now have the hero advocating for my authority." She removed the sword with its sheath from the belt and presented it to her uncle.

I wasn't happy about this. The scabbard was carved with my crest, the maiden and the spring. While the sword itself was a fine piece gifted by Rigel, the crest she so proudly thrust toward her uncle had been drawn up in a hurry and slapped on specifically for my appointment ceremony. While it looked fine from afar, anyone could see how crude it was up close. The field marshal's honor was at stake here.

"I have sworn my service to the hero," she continued. "As you can see, he has bestowed his sword upon me. No one would dare reject my authority now. Any lords who voice their objections may be burned in the flames of Veralgon."

Hold up, I don't remember saying you could keep th—wait, what are you saying I'll do?

Her words left Gordan dumbfounded as well. He turned and lashed out at me with a dreadful look in his eyes. "Hero! What exactly have you been teaching my niece?! What do you think you're doing, coming here and..."

I didn't quite know how to respond. In fact, I wanted an explanation for what was going on just as much as he did.

He quickly picked up on my confusion and realized what was going on. Just like that, his anger subsided, and he staggered over to a nearby bench.

"That's enough. Just do whatever you want, Meg."

Megriel smiled from ear to ear with glee, looking almost as if she was about to start jumping up and down on the spot. "Thanks, Uncle! Well, then, I should go and greet the retinue!"

Taking her uncle's two guards along with her, she began to sprint away, but she stopped and turned back for a moment when they reached the door. "Oh, look after my uncle, would you?"

Gordan is already wiped out. How am I supposed to help?

"And Uncle, you hurry and recover. There are loads of things I need your help with." Waving, she continued on, her smile as radiant as ever.

"I've had enough of this! I'm retiring!" Gordan screamed, but the thick doors were already shut tight behind her.

Gordan slumped down on the bench, his head drooping. I took a seat next to him.

"I'm sure my niece has caused you all sorts of trouble." His voice was faint.

"Likewise. It looks like I've done something I shouldn't have."

He shook his head at my apology. "It's nothing to fault you for. No doubt it was a carefully planned act."

Thinking back on it now, there were a number of things that didn't make sense. I was the one who had waved them all away. We shared a deep sigh.

For a while, silence reigned. Then the sudden sound of men cheering came from the yard. Gordan raised his face ever so slightly in that direction. "If only that one had been born a man, all our troubles would fade away," he muttered and then fell back into his slump.

"Might I hear the circumstances?"

It was uncouth to pry into another house's business, but when I was dragged so far into it, surely I had the right to know a little bit.

Turning his powerless eyes to me, he answered my question with a question. "Have you ever met my brother? I believe you were stationed together in the last battle."

His brother would be Megriel's father. His name was... What was he called again? *Oh. She called herself the daughter of Cardon.* But which one was he? The day after I was summoned, I had been introduced to all the key players at the same time, so surely, I couldn't be expected to remember them all. After our defeat, I was sure I'd never see them again, so I never bothered to try.

"I'm sorry. That was when I had only just been summoned to this world, and—" Just then, I recalled him: He was the man who'd led the main force during the decisive battle—the one in the flashy armor. "No, I remember him! He was wearing bright-red armor."

"Yeah, that's him. My brother."

Good. I got it right.

"My brother was a born fighter. He would form a subjugation force every year to attack orc territory." Gordan had a lonesome smile on his face. "He was known from a young age for his strength. He would always return with plenty of spoils. On top of all that, he was such a good speaker. His tales of adventure would get everyone's heart racing, and they would listen in a trance. The territory flourished, and the name of Morsharz spread."

He sounds proud when he speaks of his brother.

"It was Megriel who enjoyed her father's stories the most. All through the winter, she would badger my brother to tell her stories of war. At the end of each one, she would say, 'I'm going to be like you!' Everyone, me included, saw her as an adorable young lass who loved her father."

He let out a sigh.

"My brother was delighted, of course. He began teaching the young girl how to fight and ride a horse. That was before Odon was born. Everyone thought, 'His attention will turn elsewhere once he has a son,' 'It's good for her to learn the basics of swords and horses,' and so on. It didn't seem like a problem. Yet by the time Odon the heir was born, Megriel had gotten so skilled that even older men were no match for her. My brother found it all incredibly amusing, but the girl's mother could hardly agree; she even discussed it with our mothers. Fortunately, that was when the palace sent a letter requesting Megriel's service. They accepted in the hopes of teaching her some manners."

The more he went on, the more pensive his expression became.

"It didn't work out. That was around the time the previous king and queen died, you see. The royal courts had become a veritable nest of vipers, and everyone had their own hidden intentions. Attention fastened on the young children His Majesty left behind, with bets placed and schemes hatched. And in the end, a few lives were lost. Ultimately, a compromise was reached between the various factions. Two military men who had kept their distance from the power struggles were chosen to nurse them. The first was Herbert, who had risen from a mercenary to an influential position in the royal army. The second, Rigel, had conceded his position as dragon rider captain to his son, and he'd essentially retired by then."

Gordan looked at the door reproachfully. Beyond it was the yard, where Rigel was with the two dragons.

"Sir Rigel is not to blame. The two of them worked hard to keep the children safe from the schemes of the palace, and they succeeded. But the two of them boasted far too many military exploits—and had too many stories to tell."

"Oh...that's unfortunate."

I could imagine those two telling the young king and princess their tales, entirely without any ill intent. And of course, there was Megriel listening right alongside them.

"You know how the princess was. She took quite a liking to Megriel and doted on her. Megriel was greatly influenced by her. Need I even spell out the result? Worse yet, through Megriel, my brother got to know the princess's character, and he was head over heels—no, not like that. I mean as a warrior."

"I understand."

The princess carried a martial charisma that drew everyone to her. It was inevitable that Megriel's father, a natural born fighter, was drawn to her.

"Once Liana came of age, Megriel was relieved from her post, and she returned to the territory. We were all hoping that she would learn some etiquette at the palace and perhaps gain some awareness of herself as a noble lady. What we got was the exact opposite. Her sword was polished even further, and only a handful of the retinue could match her. There wasn't a single one who could defeat her in a joust. Everyone lamented what could have been had she been born a man."

The daughter they sent off hoping she might return a lady came back even more delinquent than before.

"My brother became so devoted to the princess that he hardly stopped to consider matters of the house. He got his old war buddies together and campaigned for the princess to become head of the Knights Templar—he even recommended her for the position of field marshal. He would answer any summons from Her Highness with the entirety of Morsharz's army. The plunder no longer interested him; he just wanted to face the orc armies alongside the princess. Naturally, the army's expenditures grew, and he had no gains to show for it. I wound up running around overseeing the territory in his stead. I somehow managed to procure money for his expeditions, calm down the lesser lords who were bearing the burden, and train up young knights to replenish the dwindling members of his retinue."

His wrinkles grew deeper as he recalled his troubles.

"Even my brother wouldn't bring Megriel into orcish lands, and the child was incredibly displeased by that. I tried to distract her by getting her to help me manage the territory. That worked out, to some degree. Megriel exhibited some talent in domestic affairs. Before long, I could leave it all to her. It was due to her that we had enough funds to hire mercenaries to cover our losses, and I was able to concentrate on training the knights. As you can see, I've finally managed to rebuild the Morsharz Retinue, considered to be elites among elites."

I could see the pride in Gordan's expression. *But seriously, what exactly is Megriel? She isn't an otherworlder too, is she? She seems far more high-spec than me.*

"The retinue will be able to march into battle next year. The restructuring of our budget is starting to bear fruit. And just as I thought everything was going well..." He stopped.

"You heard your brother had died in the last battle," I finished for him.

"Yes."

"I'm sorry I wasn't able to save him."

"Don't be. Lives are lost even in a winning battle. That is the fate of all warriors. No one holds it against you. That said, it in essence put us in quite a predicament. Odon was still young, and Megriel was a woman. Sure, everyone who knew her would have accepted her as the successor, but it was clear that the lords under us wouldn't agree. I left the work to Megriel, as I had already been doing, while posing as the land's protector to quell the chaos."

"She said you confined her in a tower," I suggested timidly.

That got a mocking laugh. "No one can lock that girl up."

As I thought.

"At first, she agreed with those conditions. But she must have been dissatisfied at her lack of military authority—the right to summon and command the armies of the lesser lords. That right could only rest with the official protector."

Even if she gathered soldiers in her uncle's name, she wouldn't be able to give them orders. That was why her uncle was the public protector to begin with.

"I'm sure she's been looking for her opportunity. She disappeared last night with Odon. I'm sure you know what happened after that better than me."

We shared another sigh.

Suddenly, the door burst open. Megriel was back. She was followed by two youths—not the same guards as before. I recognized them as the knights that were chasing her when we first met.

"This is Chrost, and this is Ekmas," she reminded me. "They're the two in the retinue I count on the most."

The two of them bowed.

"I beg you to overlook my prior discourtesy."

"Likewise, my apologies."

"They were acting on my orders. Please be lenient with them." Megriel lowered her head alongside them. *Impressive. Is that why they followed her?*

"Forget about it," I said. "How did you know I was coming?"

"Yesterday, a kind person told me that a dragon rider came to ready the place for someone important."

I couldn't take this "kind person" at face value.

"So you were lying in wait for me?"

"Yes. If the hero was going to see his territory, I knew he would have to visit the temple."

I was a puppet dancing in her palm.

"Incidentally, Hero, can't you do something about the way you speak?"

She was suddenly chastising me for my speech. What was strange about it? My hero's power translated my words to the language of whatever world I was in. I didn't know how accurate it was, but I hadn't run into any obvious problems. My tutor didn't have much to say about my etiquette in that regard.

"Is there something wrong with how I speak?"

"I don't mind if you use that tone with Sir Rigel or Torson, but you shouldn't be speaking so cordially with your vassals."

A vassal is lecturing me for being too polite.

"Why?"

"The hero will be made light of if he can't manage a woman. If my lord is looked down upon, I will be too."

That's the truth, though. I can't manage her.

"Megriel. You've got the position you wanted. Can't we forget that vow ever happened?"

Honestly, I was tired. I didn't want to get involved. I got the feeling I'd be dragged into even more trouble.

"Call me Meg. I wouldn't dream of annulling our vows. Why, I've just renewed them in my heart, knowing I'll have to return the favor someday."

This brazen little...

"They were made under false pretenses. Those vows should be invalid."

"There was just a bit of theatrics involved. The hero shall protect me. I shall serve him. That's all there is to it. Neither of us has broken it! Oh, but service in this case is limited to military service. No strange ideas, okay?"

"Yeah, not happening."

I'm more scared of what she would do to me!

"If you ever go out to battle, please invite me. We'll all gladly fight alongside you."

She got down on one knee and lowered her head. *Gladly, huh? I see. This was where her ambition really began.*

"Perhaps this was for the best," Gordan muttered.

"What do you mean?"

"I always thought it was a pity for her talents to go to waste.

I'm sure she will be able to make use of her resourcefulness under the hero."

Perhaps that was the case. If she was a competent general, it would no doubt be a plus to humanity. But there was a problem. I was the one who would need to clean up after this mess. Not him. No doubt that serene look on Gordan's face came from knowing he had been liberated from all his troubles. He thought everything was about to be wrapped up in a pretty little bow. *Nope, not on my watch.*

"Sir Gordan."

"Yes, Hero?"

"I do not permit your retirement. Keep us company a bit longer. That is my condition."

He rose from the bench, got down on one knee, and lowered his head.

"Yes, sir! Understood."

"Meg!"

"Yes."

"I'm going to work you to the bone."

"With pleasure, my lord."

She looked me straight in the eye and smiled. As always, it was a fine smile that made me want to protect it. But surely there was no need. She was entirely able to protect herself—dragging in everyone around her as she did so.

Early the next morning, Rigel and I returned to the manor on Kadann Hill. I led Veralgon to the dragon house only to find it was already occupied by an unfamiliar dragon with indigo wings. Noticing we had returned, Torson rushed out of the manor.

"Hero! We've received an urgent notice from the capital!"

There was a dragon rider behind him who must have brought the message.

"What happened?" I said.

"Yesterday, Dragonjaw Gate was attacked by the orc army. The defensive barrier was destroyed! His Majesty commands you to report there at once!"

CHAPTER 6

A DRAGON'S FLAMES

EVEN THE BLACK DOG was dumbfounded by the scene that unfolded before his eyes near Dragonjaw Gate. The eight massive siege cannons he had gone through such great lengths to transport had managed to break through the humans' defensive barrier, but the thrill of victory lasted for only a moment. The settling sands suddenly turned to a muddy stream that swallowed everything in its path.

The legends were true... The Black Dog groaned. In the margrave's land, there was an old tale of a water dragon from the valley pushing back an attacking army. He watched as the massive dragon of stone—Dragonjaw Gate's sluice gate—continued expelling a thundering torrent.

Luckily, his own men, the aquilup riders, were safe. Aquilups were beasts who lived in steep, treacherous mountains; they could run up the valley's slopes with little effort to escape the danger. However, the cannoneers and the foot soldiers guarding them were nearly all swept away. It wasn't hard to imagine what became of their cannons.

Was the margrave's army safe where it was deployed at the mouth of the valley? The Black Dog turned to look, but they weren't visible from where he stood. They were probably fine, he thought. They would have been able to see the water coming. Even in his absence, someone with good sense would give the retreat order. Unlike his motherland's main army, fortified with far too many pointless nobles, the margrave's army was never lacking in talent. Their strength was forged in frequent battles with the humans.

While the army's safety weighed heavily on his mind, there was nothing he could do until the water subsided. He glanced at the muddy stream passing beneath him. He could see a few lucky soldiers who had found handholds clinging on for dear life on its edge. He at least had to do what he could. He commanded his riders to save them.

They made it back to their main force the next morning. The troops had suffered hardly any losses. The commissioned officers had quickly realized something was wrong and issued the appropriate orders.

Unfortunately, their facilities had suffered serious damage. More than half of the fences they had set up to impede a cavalry charge were washed away, and worse, their supplies were in a dreadful state. The biggest problem would be the gunpowder, much of which was now completely useless. According to the officers, it would be difficult to hold the line if they were attacked on the same scale as the last great battle.

Should we retreat, then? The thought crossed his mind, but he rejected it. *No, it shouldn't be an issue. They can't send their armored cavalry until the mud dries. We have plenty of time. Now we just wait for replenishments.*

He did have one fear: the dragons that the humans employed. For some reason, they had been absent from the last battle, but recently, there had been reports of sightings here and there. Usually they were somewhat manageable, but it would be a completely different story without gunpowder. Right now, it would be the worst possible scenario if those flying beasts came back in full force.

But the Black Dog shelved that thought. Even without gunpowder, they would be able to defend themselves. Attacks from the sky would inflict damage, but they would not be enough to drive the orc legions away. It wasn't an issue.

He instructed his men to draft a supply request and then headed off to see the soldiers. When they saw that the Black Dog was unharmed, surely that would boost their falling morale.

•❘✳❘•

The narrow path leading from Dragonjaw Gate into orcish territory was filled to the brim with mud. The orcs had already pulled out, and there was no movement to be seen. Luckily, the gate itself was still in one piece, but the water level behind the dam—previously at its peak—had gone down considerably. Herbert had opened the sluice gates to attack the orcs who were closing in.

When I was sure there were no orcs around, I cautiously lowered my altitude. Rigel had warned me to be careful of skilled orc snipers when flying low. I immediately found what I was looking for—a smokestack sprouting straight out of the mud. I'd heard there had been ten of them in total, but I only saw three. The rest were most likely buried.

I rose up again, this time making for the mouth of the valley. The orcs stationed outside of the valley must have been hit hard by the water that surged through it. If we were lucky, maybe the whole army had been swept away.

But my hopes were quickly dashed; the orcs were still in fine condition. Part of their palisades was destroyed, but that was it. An uncountable number of them was still parked right outside the valley. I could see orcs in the forest cutting down trees to rebuild their defenses.

They were not assembled in formation, so their numbers were difficult to assess, but from what I could tell, they hadn't gone down by much. Upon seeing me, some of them organized themselves and aimed their guns. They were brimming with fighting spirit. No doubt they were going to stay right where they were.

They didn't shoot, which told me I was out of range, but I knew I shouldn't get any closer. For the time being, I'd seen what I could see. I set course north to return to Dragonjaw Gate.

The atmosphere was suffocating in the room where the defense meeting was about to begin. Five men sat around the round table. There was His Majesty, of course, and Rigel, the dragon riders' captain. Also attending was Herbert, who led Dragonjaw's garrison. Then there was Fargas—an unfamiliar face—the new captain of the Knights Templar. The fifth man at the table was yours truly, the hero-slash-field marshal. While the captain of the royal guard was also present, he stood directly behind His Majesty—a guard rather than a participant.

Officially, this meeting was being overseen by the field marshal. I was supposed to invite the main lords, but given the circumstances, it would take time for them to arrive from their territories. And honestly, would they even come on my summons? Meg was still out swinging around the sword with my crest on it, rallying the lords in her domain.

"In this offensive, the orcs unveiled cannons bigger than any we have ever seen. They stationed them around here."

Herbert indicated a point on the map that was spread out on the table. It was about midway up the valley and two kilometers from the gate.

"They had roughly ten cannons. It took half a day to ready them. The bombardment began around noon, and while the gate's magic barrier withstood the first volley, it was shattered on the second. Our walls have taken some damage. There appears to be a one-hour window between their shots."

"In just two volleys?!"

Fargas sounded like he could hardly believe it. I'd arrived early thanks to my dragon and received a report in advance, but he had only just arrived with His Majesty, so this was news to him.

"Determining that it was a national crisis, I immediately opened the floodgates. The water managed to sweep away all the orcs in the valley, as well as a portion of the encampment outside. Since then, the orcs have shown no signs of preparing for another attack."

"Herbert, can I assume that we've succeeded in our defense?" Despite his words, Fargas's expression was not optimistic.

"Yes, against yesterday's attack, at least. However, Dragonjaw Gate is still in a critical state." The look on Herbert's face turned grim. "We used more than half of our stored water in the discharge. The level won't recover until snowmelt season. Perhaps we'll be able to wash away the enemy one more time, but after that, we'll be forced to protect ourselves with arrows. The barrier has yet to recover, and it will be a harsh battle even without their cannons."

There were several problems. In the first place, there weren't many soldiers stationed at the gate, since the orcs hadn't attacked it for the past two hundred years. Then, the orc cannons were buried, not destroyed, and could possibly be restored. Even those massive walls wouldn't come out unscathed if they were fired upon without their magic barrier.

"How long until the barrier can be deployed again?" My question prompted Herbert to glance at Fargas. Magic fell under the temple's jurisdiction.

"Through repeated investigations, the scholars do have a fairly firm grasp on the workings of the magic circle," Fargas answered. "We believe it might be possible to reactivate it, but we would have to gather over two thousand priests to do so. That will take some time."

"Might?"

"Yes, the procedure is still highly speculative. It would be our first time conducting the ceremony."

Are we going to be all right? Come to think of it, they said that was the first time the barriers had ever been broken since a magician built the fortress in the distant past. I should be grateful they even studied it.

"We'll need to force them to retreat before they can prepare for the next attack," Rigel said. They all nodded, but did any of them really know how they would do that? "A frontal assault would be...reckless." Again, nods all around.

But wait. We had forces that hadn't been available last time around.

"What about the dragons?" I said. "Can't we burn them from the sky?"

"Hero, it appears your appraisal of our dragon riders is a bit unrealistic," Fargas said with a snort. "Indeed, they may be able to easily burn our own armies to the ground. But they are useless against orcs. At most, they can do menial tasks—scouting and carrying messages."

"Silence! Are you making light of the dragon riders?!" Rigel bellowed, jumping to his feet. His clenched fists were quivering, and the veins on his temples throbbed.

"Now, now. Calm down. Scouting and communication are some of the most important roles in the army," I said.

My attempt to soothe him seemed to have little effect on his rage, and Fargas poured fuel on the flames.

"If you want to prove me wrong, go ahead, show us some evidence," he said. "I know you've got nothing." *This man must really hate Rigel,* I thought.

"Then what about you?! How about you show me how useful your bald greenhorns can be!"

"Don't be an idiot. The situation is different for our Knights Templar. Had Liana not recklessly charged and expended them, they would still be doing their part as the hero's trump card."

"Now you're insulting the princess too! Have you no shame?!" Rigel drew his sword. "Take up your blade! You'll pay for those words!"

That sword was Rigel's pride. I'd heard that it was made of pure silver from tip to pommel, but did that really make it any better as a blade? Fargas grinned as he reached for his own weapon. *They're really going to do it!*

"Cease this! Both of you!" the king roared. "How dare you hold such trifling personal squabbles in my presence!" His voice was far louder than what I thought possible from someone so small.

"My apologies, Sire." Fargas bowed and then took his seat again. "You too, dragon man. Sheathe your weapon."

Rigel glared at Fargas for a moment, and then, clearly reluctant, tucked away his blade. With some urging from His Majesty, he took his seat.

"Uh, so why are dragon riders useless against orcs?" I asked timidly. I knew it was a bad idea to bring it up again, but I simply had to know.

With a gleeful expression, Fargas opened his mouth to speak, but His Highness silenced him with a glance. "Rigel," the king said. "Please explain it to him."

"Certainly, sir." Vexation flitted across his face, but he quickly composed himself. Looking me straight in the eye, he said, "The reason is simple. The orcs have advanced the might of their guns to the point where their range just exceeds that of a dragon's fiery breath. With their close-knit formations, an approach from the sky amounts to suicide."

"I see. Then that rules out a dragon rider charge."

Well, anyone could have thought of that. There'd be no point in the king calling this meeting if that was all it took.

"Please, Hero, don't think that the dragon riders are completely useless!" Rigel's eyes were bloodshot. "If we attack with our entire force, a third of them may be able to get close enough to rain fire! Those who fall will crash into the enemy formation and create a gap that we can take advantage of! Send our horses in through there, and we can tear the enemy formation apart!"

"Y-yes, I'll...keep that in mind." I stammered. *There are plenty of ways to use dragons. Why waste them as disposable missiles?*

"Easy now, Rigel," Herbert said. The room was silent as Rigel caught his breath.

So no one even had anything else to suggest? No, I did have one idea. The problem was, I didn't know how effective it would be, and I didn't even want to think about what would happen afterward. Still, we had to do something about the crisis we were facing.

"I have a plan." All eyes turned to me. "Please place the dragon riders under my command. I guarantee that I will drive the enemy away."

I didn't know if it would work, but it was better than doing nothing. A disheartened Rigel looked at me, eyes filled with expectation. Fargas, in contrast, stared at me doubtfully.

"Is that all right, Rigel?" His Majesty asked.

"Yes, sire! Please use us however you see fit! We will certainly prove our worth!"

'ᚢᚢ'

The winds were rough in the skies above Dragonbone Ridge. The mountains were always coiled in violent turbulence when winter came. Kyel suppressed the temptation to sink his face into warm dragon plumage, keeping his eyes looking forward. A bone-chilling wind peppered with ice scraped across his cheek.

A sudden downdraft forced him and his dragon to drop altitude. Just as quickly, their right wing was dragged upward. He concentrated hard to keep them from veering left. The mountain currents were fickle, and they never let up. It was impossible for riders flying side by side to stay in formation. Honestly, he could hardly keep on course. It took a toll on the dragon too—usually not even wild dragons flew this high.

What's more, it was the time of year when wild dragons entered hibernation. Whomever had ordered them to fly over Dragonbone Ridge at this time of year must have lost his mind. In fact, the man who'd given that order was right there, flying at the forefront, unflinching through the storm.

"He's a monster," Kyel muttered.

Kyel's father had been a dragon rider, and his father before him. The talent to ride was not hereditary, and it was exceedingly rare for it to appear in three generations. His grandfather could tell so many tales of his adventures, and he was now a great rider and the captain of the force. Kyel's father, who had also served as captain, was a genius who had managed to ride Veralgon. Kyel knew that great things were expected of him, but he had been unable to become anyone special. Even so, he dreamed of riding that white dragon one day, just like his father. He worked tirelessly toward this dream.

Then Veralgon had been snatched up by that man who had appeared out of nowhere. His grandfather Rigel had always been harsh on him. Since the day he found out he had the talent to be a rider, he remembered being complimented only a handful of times. Yet his grandfather was all over that man, going on and on about how he was God's chosen hero. Kyel could not sympathize, as he did not believe in God as strongly as his grandfather did. It simply felt like that man had stolen not only his father's dragon but his grandfather's love as well.

Kyel shook those thoughts from his head. He couldn't deny that man's abilities. He could fly undeterred through violent airstreams and handled Veralgon like a master. Dragons cared nothing for the titles the temple bestowed. They knew only skill.

His body was lifted up again and then violently smacked downward only a few moments later. He was losing height like he had gone into a nosedive. They had already left the tree line far behind them, and bare crags were approaching right before his eyes. Gravity vanished, and as his body nearly left the saddle, only his lifeline was holding him. As he regained control, he lifted the dragon's head and had it flap to ascend. That took a toll on the dragon, but he needed to regain the lost altitude.

"Concentrate. Don't let it get to you," he told himself. For now, he had to concentrate on flying.

The man at the front began rising even higher. A conspicuously higher ridge line was approaching. Once they crossed, they would be over level ground. Just one more push. Kyel signaled for the dragon to flap even harder. He could feel intense fatigue, though it wasn't his own; the dragon was worn out. The feeling was so strong that Kyel could sense it, even though he was far from reaching unity of soul.

I worked so hard, and yet... Thinking about the mission that awaited him beyond the mountains, he felt entirely unmotivated. His colleagues were likely the same. This was not a job for dragon riders. It was a dragon rider's duty to attack an enemy from the sky, burning holes in their lines. However, they'd had very few opportunities to carry out that duty these past few years. They were given backline roles—recon, communications, patrol. This time, they'd been given a new odd job.

Now they have us burning down a trifling orc village.

Kyel couldn't comprehend why his proud grandfather, the model dragon rider, had accepted the mission.

◆

"We will burn down the orc villages."

Rigel looked at me somberly. "Just burn them?"

The conference was over and we were the only ones remaining. His sorrowful voice rang through the empty room.

"Yes, and the wagons too." I kept it brief.

"May I ask why?"

"We can't win this battle. Instead, we will attack their supply chain to force them to retreat."

"Don't get me wrong, I understand your intentions. They will no doubt have to pull back once their provisions are cut off. But why us?"

What was he trying to say? If he understood that much, then wasn't the rest obvious?

"Because the dragon riders are the only ones who can do it," I told him. "Now that the valley is closed off, only the dragon riders can fly over their heads and attack what's behind them."

While His Majesty had given me the right to command the military, Rigel was the only one who could order the dragon riders, and the only one they would obey. I would need to convince him.

"I get what you're saying, Hero, but the orc villagers are a source of income for the lords. Burning them may reduce our yields for years to come. Also, if we are launching an attack from Dragonjaw Gate, there are no longer any notable villages within flying distance. Not to mention—" He paused briefly. "A dragon rider's role is to launch a powerful assault in battle. If we start burning orc nests... A proud dragon rider should never go around playing pyromaniac! I am reluctant to put the riders up to something of that caliber."

He had lined up various reasons, but I suspected he only really cared about the last one. His tone of voice had changed toward the end. So that was the stumbling block for Rigel—and for the dragon riders. Now that I knew that, there was room for negotiation.

"It might be a trifling mission compared to their usual work, but please think of the results it will bring."

His eyebrows were sagging in despair. Now they twitched. I had his interest.

"If the dragon riders' work manages to remove the orcish legions, then what?" I pressed. "Your riders will have managed to pull off what the allied armies and Knights Templar put together couldn't do."

His brow wrinkled in thought, and after a while, he spoke. "Of course, the merits will be significant. But the dragon riders' pride... Those with pride must not wield their powers unjustly. Fighting an army is one thing, but I do not like the idea of turning our flames toward the defenseless—orcs though they may be."

"Armed or not, an orc is an orc. Isn't destroying the orcs the mission of every knight?"

"Indeed, it is our God-given duty."

"Then you must sever the problem at the root. Using the dragon riders for this purpose might be like using an axe to sever a sewing thread, but it is nothing shameful in the eyes of God."

"Y-yes, but..." Rigel hung his head, but I had him rattled. I just needed to make one more push.

"Please think of those who fell to the orcs," I said. "Would Princess Liana want those orcs to remain in that valley?"

His shoulders pricked up the moment I mentioned Liana's name. That really got him going. I decided to rile him up more.

"The princess was not the only one killed. For their sake, we must have our vengeance. A baptism by flames!"

As I recalled, he had lost his son to the orcs too.

"It is the wrath of God! They must know his fiery rage! Let the flames of vengeance burn them to the ground! Send them cowering in fear! Have them remember us every time they see a lit match! Is it clouds that dominate the sky? Nay, it is the flocks of dragons! The glimmering sun is a dragon's flames!"

Even I didn't know what I was saying by this point.

"Hero!" Rigel suddenly stood. His whole body quivered as he looked straight at me. "Let's do it! The skies are on our side! We'll teach them a lesson."

Dragon fire burned in his eyes. But damn, that old man sure was a pushover. I was starting to get worried about him.

A month had passed since we first implemented our scorched-earth tactics. Fall was coming to an end, and winter was about to begin.

We had decided to split the riders into two forces. One aimed for supply caravans coming from orc territory, and the other aimed for the villages—their lifeline in these lands. Rigel took charge of the caravans, and I took the villages. Giving him the more interesting job was the least I could do.

But Rigel faced a setback even before the first week was over. The wagons used to come a few at a time, but they quickly learned to send several dozen together, armed with powerful guards to defend them from the dragon rider attacks. If he accepted some sacrifices, he would be able to destroy these new larger supply caravans. But dragons and riders were too valuable and too hard to replace; I wasn't going to waste them like that. I ordered him to only attack caravans that were lightly guarded.

Meanwhile, things weren't going so smoothly with my own unit either. We'd started off using Dragonjaw Gate as our base of operations. It was closer to the other side of the mountains, which saved us the trouble of the long crossing. Unfortunately, by the second day, we had already burned through every village within a day's flight. The area had already been plundered dry by the subjugation forces, and there hadn't been any important villages left anyway.

If we wanted to make further impact, we would have to encroach deeper into orc territory, but that was out of the question. If the orc forces attacked us while we were close to the ground, even dragon riders stood no chance. To ensure our own safety, we had to fly too high for their bullets to reach.

With little choice in the matter, we were forced to sail over Dragonbone Ridge from other points. Crossing those mountains was surprisingly taxing. We would have to cross before the sun came up, fulfill our objective without rest, and head back before sunset to return to the base. Even though we chose the lowest and most spacious places to cross, most dragons would wind up so tired that they couldn't fly the next day. Even Veralgon could only keep his attacks up for three days tops.

The riders also quickly became exhausted—except for me, with my enhanced hero's body. When Veralgon wasn't available, I would borrow dragons whose riders were resting. Soon, the riders who at first looked at me with respect began to see me as a monster. As time passed, more and more of the riders needed long periods of rest. After a month, the caravan and village teams had only eight riders in working condition between them.

I was crossing the mountains again with three of the valuable eight. Veralgon was resting, so I was riding a dragon with moss-green wings who was my usual alternative. He was a young one, conceived in the last breeding season twelve years ago, and he was quite a bit lighter than Veralgon and far less stable in the turbulence. However, he was docile by nature, so he would fly straight so long as I properly took control, and his youth meant he recovered quickly.

A thick forest spread out southwest of the mountains, then thinned as it was replaced by a wasteland of exposed rock. At times, I would spot a small woodland or a burnt settlement. My plan had succeeded. No villages remained intact anywhere near the mountain ridge. I sent a signal for my colleagues to disperse. The riders watched for one another's hand signals and got into a search formation. We pressed farther and farther into orc territory.

But as far as we went, it was the same forests and wastelands below. Not a single orc village was left standing. I'd had my eye on a village on my way back the previous day, but it was already burned down by the time I returned to it. Perhaps they packed up their winter stocks and evacuated before we could get to them. But even if they had, I doubted they would set it on fire of their own accord.

When I looked to the sky, I saw the sun had climbed to almost its peak. We would need to cross back by sunset, so it was about time to pull out. I felt we could probably declare this operation complete. We had apparently burned down every village within range. Hardly any of the dragon riders were in any condition to fly, and what's more, winter was coming. Soon, the turbulence would get even worse. There was no point in persisting.

Once we got back to base, I would bring the operation to a close. It was quite a depressing notion. The orcs were still squatting at the valley's entrance, despite how hard I'd worked the riders. I was sure they must resent me. Rigel still supported me, but not his subordinates. They wouldn't go along with my unreasonable demands after this.

The sun finally reached its zenith. It was time.

Just then, the rider to the right of me sent a signal. He had spotted a village. I checked the sun again and calculated the time we had left. We would just barely make it. It would be a bit dangerous, but better than returning with nothing to show for it. I signaled for the spotter to lead the way, and for the other riders to group.

The dragon at the lead had feathers that looked orange from a distance but were actually a vivid array of red and gold. He was definitely the most accomplished of the bunch. His rider was called Kyel, as I recalled. He was the youngest dragon rider and Rigel's one and only grandson. His colleagues had dropped out one after another, but he was still in flying condition, probably thanks to his youth. While his first flight over the mountains had been a rough one, he was now more stable than anyone. He had grown commendably. Surely, he would one day become a first-rate rider and even surpass Rigel.

We arrived at the airspace above the village. The dragons spread out, circling overhead. On my signal, the four dragons roared in unison. The orcs fled their houses in a commotion. Once they were fully aware of us, I ordered the attack. The reason I gave them time to evacuate was not an ethical one; it was to create as many refugees as possible. Once they had lost their beds and food for the winter, they would have to seek shelter elsewhere. The farming villages would be unable to accommodate them. They would have no choice but to make the trek to the orc cities where more food was stored. The need to feed these refugees would reduce the supplies that could be provided to the military. Some might even flee to the army for safety. I'd heard reports from Rigel of evacuees sighted heading for the garrisons.

And if instead, the orc statesmen refused to give them food, leaving them to die, that saved me the trouble of killing them.

We dropped altitude as we circled. I saw the orcs race back into their houses. I'd gone out of my way to give them a warning. What were they trying to do? Had they built bunkers under their houses? Perhaps they were simply incapable of making rational decisions. As we lowered to attack height, each rider locked on to a building and proceeded straight for it.

Something was wrong. I felt a foul chill on my back. I didn't know if it was part of my hero skill set, but that chill had saved me before in a number of worlds. Immediately, I had the dragon roll and make a sharp turn. The next instant...

Bang!

The straw flew off the thatch roof of the house I was headed for. Something glimmering passed through the space where I had been a moment ago.

I had the dragon flap to gain height.

Boom!

A second shot from a different direction. The roofless houses were shrinking in my field of view, and now I saw what had blown them away: cannons. Inside each exposed room, the orcs were aiming long cannons with fuses up at us. The glimmering object had probably been a cannister of shrapnel shot from the barrel.

I directed the dragon to somersault in the air, changing course straight for a cannon and dropping into a nosedive. The orcs dropped their tools and scattered. I peppered the ground with fire, maintaining my speed as I flew parallel to the ground. Then, I deployed a barrier behind me and was met by a massive explosion. They must have been storing the cannon powder in one of the rooms I'd hit. Fragments of all sizes grated against my barrier. They struck the dragon's wings, and it recoiled from the pain. Luckily, it didn't suffer any major injuries.

I pressed on for a while, ascending again once I was a safe distance from the village, and then turned back. The first thing I saw was the gap left by a house, blown away without a trace. Then, a dark-blue dragon that had survived the counterattack. Then, a group of orc gunmen getting into formation in the village plaza. There were over a hundred of them. Finally, I saw the dragon with the intricate orange wings. He was safe. But we were one dragon short.

Dammit!

I heard explosions from at least two places. There had to be another cannon. But where? I locked on to another house without a roof on the opposite side of the village. I deployed a barrier in front and swooped lower, gliding just over the ground, as I used other houses as shields to approach where I thought the cannon was. We gained speed each time the dragon's wings scraped through the air. Trees and buildings shot past—so close that I could nearly reach out and touch them.

Here! I rose up a block before the building in question. With a barrel roll, I drew a spiral in the air, turning my neck to the limit to capture my target in my sights. Just as I thought, there was a cannon in the house without a roof. The dragon saw it too. Its muzzle completely failed to track our movements. Just as we had with the last one, we breathed fire from above, and then I deployed a barrier behind as we fled from the blast at full force.

That did it. For now, I'd avenged the rider who fell. I failed to burn the village, but I'd preserved our honor. There wasn't much time left, and we would have to retreat before we suffered any more losses.

It happened just as I was about to give the return order. I saw the orange dragon diving toward the ground. He was headed for where the fallen dragon lay belly-up, exposing its light-gray underside.

"Stop!" I cried, but he couldn't hear from this distance.

The formation of orc soldiers pointed their guns at the swooping dragons. They locked aim. Even if I wanted to help him, there was nothing I could do from this distance.

Then came the burst.

Their square formation was cloaked in gunpowder smoke. The orange dragon must have taken a direct hit to the wings—its body lurched and it went down, drawing slow circles away from the city. That was my only chance. I had my dragon flap its wings and plunge straight into the orc formation. They had just fired, so this was my chance to approach safely.

I saw the remaining dragon swoop down as well. The orcs scattered like baby spiders from the smoke, and I chased them, showering them with flames. Each shot would send a ball of fire bursting into an orc's back.

After chasing them away, I flew back over the village to check on the orange dragon. Its rider had been thrown a short distance away. I saw him get to his feet. I looked at the other rider—his name was Oifel, as I recalled. *What do we do?* his eyes asked. I went over the situation in my head.

Cannons? I was hearing no other shots. They probably didn't have any more. The foot soldiers? In disarray, but they were already beginning to fire back.

Who was the idiot who had descended of his own accord? Kyel. Rigel's grandson.

After those brief thoughts, I signaled, "Support me." I immediately received an affirmative.

Turning my course toward the orange dragon, I lowered my speed and altitude as much as I could. In front of it, the young rider waved his arms, awaiting me. I leaned as far as I could out of the saddle, reaching out, as the dragon's circles slowly closed in. Wings spread wide, just enough speed not to stall, I altered our course ever so slightly to the right to pass by him. The roar of a dragon and gunshots echoed from the village.

I could feel the impact as the young rider jumped into my arms. *All right! Got him!*

There was a forest ahead of me. If I wanted enough speed to lift off, I would need to maintain this altitude, while moving my wings at full speed. There was just barely enough distance. Or so I thought, when suddenly, a great number of orc soldiers appeared from the trees. They seemed panicked—awfully slow to ready their guns.

The dragon's wings felt heavy. I was supposed to be moving them for dear life, but I was hardly gaining any speed. The color drained from my vision as everything turned gray. It would be impossible to evade the enemy. If I turned now, I would definitely lose my lift. The dragon's mouth opened wide to breathe fire. A whistling sound escaped its lungs. Out of fuel.

The orcs fired. Gray trails of smoke shot straight for us. I deployed a barrier, which made it in time.

All of a sudden, a pain raced through my body as my right wing was dyed red. The color and speed returned to my surroundings, and I slid across the ground as the dragon came to a halt. Its massive body dragged the orcs along before smacking into the trees.

I was thrown into the woods with the rider I'd saved.

'ᴗ'

East of Dragonbone Ridge, near an orc hamlet, Kyel saw something he couldn't believe. A moss-green dragon was speeding toward him. With so many orc gunmen on the prowl, no sane man would fly at such a low altitude.

What are you doing? Do you want to die?!

Kyel was aware that he had done something stupid. His comrade fell, and he let the blood go to his head. He had seen an orc approaching the fallen dragon, and he could see them pulling his friend's dead body out from beneath. That was when he lost control. He had no idea what he'd wanted to accomplish. After being crushed under a dragon, the man couldn't possibly have been alive; that much was obvious.

Still, he was driven by an impulse to do *something*, and he could no longer see anything other than his friend and the orcs flocking around him. Only when the bullets struck did he remember the orcs in the plaza. Kyel had been an idiot—plain and simple. He was sure he would be abandoned, yet that man was trying to save him.

Stop! That's enough! Raise your altitude!

He waved his hands trying to send that message, but the dragon's rider leaned out as if paying him no mind at all. Blinded by his own shortcomings, Kyel had labeled him a madman.

Fine! Have it your way!

He leapt into the arms approaching him. Once he was in position, the man held him lightly with one hand, accelerating his dragon toward the forest ahead. They had just barely enough distance to clear it. The road was fraught with danger, yet that man was laughing. He still smiled even when the orcs appeared ahead. Strangely enough, there wasn't a hint of madness to his eyes.

Kyel was terrified. Who could possibly enjoy this situation? The orcs fired. The dragon's wings ran red with blood, and it went down. It slid along the ground, crashing straight into the forest. Kyel was thrown again, rolling along the forest floor. He felt a jolt on his back, and the wind was knocked out of him.

I need to stand up!

Enduring the dull pain, he coughed as he hobbled to his feet, only for pain to race down his legs and his sight to veer to one side.

He fell helplessly with nothing to grab on to. His leg was pointing in an unnatural direction.

This time, it really was the end. He lay on his back, staring up at the sky. Through the trees, he saw a dragon pass by. It was probably Oifel's. It circled the forest a few times before eventually making off in the direction of Dragonbone Ridge. *Come to think of it, is the hero safe?*

He hoped so. If the hero died due to his mistake, no doubt his grandfather would give up on him for good. When that thought occurred to him, he felt a laugh starting to build up. Why was he thinking of his grandfather's face now of all times?

A rustling sound brought him to his senses. Something was breaking through the thicket. He reached for the dagger at his hip. The terrible rumors of what happened to the humans caught by orcs crossed his mind.

But what appeared was, in a sense, a face he wanted to see even less.

"What, already given up?"

Looking down over Kyel, the hero spoke with his typical smile. He usually looked so nonchalant, but for some reason, that man with the uninspired expression now had life in his eyes. His words were more casual than usual.

"Finally found you. You flew quite a long way, you know. Took a bit of time."

In his daze, he saw the hero's outstretched hand. He was about to take it when he remembered his own situation.

"I can't walk anymore. Please leave me. You need to survive."

For the first time, the hero noticed Kyel's leg. "Oh, it's pretty busted. No way you can get up like that."

"Yes, so—"

"Give me a sec. I'll make a splint."

Ignoring Kyel, the hero formed a spear of light to sever a nearby branch. Using impromptu bandages torn from his cape, he crudely fastened it to the broken leg.

"Well, it ain't pretty, but that should do for now. C'mon, I'll lend you a shoulder. Hold on."

"B-but, sir..."

While Kyel hesitated, the hero insisted there was no time and hoisted him onto his feet. The sudden movement caused even more pain.

"Ow!"

"Quiet down. There are orcs nearby."

But the hero was still smiling.

"How—" *How can you smile right now?* he wanted to ask. But he got the feeling that wasn't the right question. "Why did you save me?"

The hero's answer was simple. "Because you're Rigel's grandson."

I see. So it's thanks to my grandfather's might. It would be difficult for that man to abandon his patron's grandchild. While Kyel was a little disappointed, at the same time, he understood. That was why the man's next words took him by surprise.

"You're his grandson, and from what I've seen, you're just like the old man. Once you've made your decision, you'll never go back on it. That's the sort of guy you are. Can't go against your blood."

PLANET OF THE ORCS

"I'm not my grandfather."

"I know that. I'm not stupid enough to judge people by bloodline. Just how many worlds do you think I've been through?" He looked at Kyel with a grin. "But I know it when I look in your eyes. Trust me, that's one thing I'm good at. You've got the same eyes as that old man. You rushed in without a second thought to help a friend, didn't you? Granted, you could have gone about it better."

"I'm sorry."

"It's fine, I get it. You're still young; there's plenty to learn. Go home and let him give you an earful."

"I'm sure he'll give up on me."

"Don't worry. Rigel's not that sorta guy. Anyway, I need men like you on my side. You're worth enough to risk my life for."

Something warm was settling in Kyel's chest. No doubt he was working for self-interest, but not the sort of self-interest Kyel was used to. He finally realized the true reason behind the disappointment he felt.

If I return alive, I'm swearing my loyalty to him, he vowed to himself. But would he be able to?

"Hero, do we have any chance of surviving?"

"Of course we do," the hero answered with a fearless smile. He wasn't even breathing hard as he shouldered Kyel and moved along the uneven forest floor.

"But Oifel already left."

"Even if we had Oifel, we wouldn't be able to cross the mountains with three on one dragon. I already made sure he knows I'm alive. Rigel will send a search party tomorrow. We just have to lay low until then. Thankfully, there don't seem to be any beak-dogs. We should be able to handle the foot soldiers. You know, you should learn from Oifel. He always thinks of the best measures to save his comrades."

The situation wasn't as bad as Kyel had imagined. He grew ashamed as he realized the depths of his own pessimism.

Now, while I'd put on airs in front of Kyel, the situation frankly wasn't looking so great. First off, I didn't know whether or not Oifel would be able to get back safely. I'd seen his dragon take a few shots, and while it could still fly, it was possible that the stamina drop from the blood loss would prevent it from making it over the mountains.

Then there was the possibility of orcish reinforcements. Before the fall, I saw pink smoke rising from the edge of the village. That was probably an emergency signal. It would be difficult to run away if those beak-dogs rushed in. No matter how much my body was enhanced, I couldn't run faster than a dog or horse. And the forest we were in wasn't that large. It didn't have too many hiding places.

Meaning that we would need to gain as much distance from the village as possible.

"Hold on, we're in for a bumpy ride."

I was about to break into a run when I heard the thicket parting behind me.

Woof! Woof!

What entered my view was man's best friend—a creature that for some reason existed in every world I'd been to. But while I was feeling pleased that my favorite animal was in this world too, its bared fangs quickly made me change gears. I stuck out my right hand, filling it with mana, then manifested a spear and pierced the dog. It resembled a Shiba Inu, a rather cute one at that. It let out a final yelp and perished.

Before I had time to take a breath, two more dogs appeared. I rolled to avoid them, being mindful of Kyel on my shoulder, and sliced at the first one as soon as I was up on my feet. I heard Kyel groan, but now was hardly the time to be concerned about that. I turned and slashed the other.

Woof! Woof! Woof!

Even more barks rose from behind me, now with the oinking sounds of the orcs mixed in. This was exceedingly bad. If I spent too much time on the dogs, the orcs would catch up. I ran off at full speed. Now was no time to show consideration for the package on my shoulder. I felt Kyel's arm around my neck tense up. Unfortunately, before we'd gone ten paces, a new dog caught up to us.

I used its barking and footsteps to judge the distance, closing in and slashing over my shoulder. The legless dog fell to the ground with a yelp, and just as I circled around to land the final blow, five more of them burst through the thicket.

These newcomers circled me at a distance, barking their heads off. They didn't go for me unless I tried to run, whereupon they would attack from behind. When I tried to strike them, they would evade me, keeping their distance and making a racket. Judging by their coordinated movements, they were clearly trained hunting dogs. Their purpose was to stall prey until the hunters arrived.

Not only was I moving slowly thanks to having Kyel on my shoulder, but I only had one free hand. I hurled a spear in irritation, but it was easily sidestepped. Seeing that I was now unarmed, the dogs rushed me all at once. I swiftly produced another spear and managed to slice one down. In that same swing, I tossed it through another.

Undeterred by the death of their comrades, the remaining three circled me, barking madly. They were good working dogs. I wished I could bring them back with me, but that wasn't going to happen.

Still, my chances were better now that there were fewer of them. I manifested a spear and cut at the nearest one. It was dodged, and I immediately turned and tossed it at another. Dodged all the same. But that broke the encirclement. I dashed with all my might into the gap.

The third one lashed out at my exposed back, as I'd expected. Luckily, Kyel blocked the attack, allowing me to impale it with a new spear without having to look back. Only two left. I could deal with two on the run.

Yet the moment that optimistic thought crossed my mind, that old chill pierced through me. I threw my body to the ground and a fuselage of gunshots burst from behind me, several dozen bullets whizzing overhead. I heard the trunks of trees splitting open and the sound of pitiful yelps. The dogs had been caught in the crossfire.

I ran. I didn't have a moment to lose. If that was all the guns they had, I would be safe for a while. I could hear the orcs squealing angrily in my direction. As I ran, I focused my ears behind me. My enhanced hearing picked out the orc with the loudest voice among them, and I concentrated.

Oink! Oooiink! Oi—

Focusing on that commanding voice, I threw my spear. At the same time, I leapt into the shadow of a tree I'd been eyeing. One breath later, I heard the disjointed *ba-ba-ba-ba-bang* of gunshots. The trunk of the tree split and leaves, twigs, and bullets flew all around.

I didn't know whether or not my spear had found its mark, but their lack of coordination meant that at least I'd caused a bit of confusion. I sprang up again. When I focused my ears, I didn't hear that well-projected tone. I manifested a shield of light instead of a spear, turning it behind me in preparation for more bullets.

Bang! Bang! Sporadic shots from behind were met with *pings* as they glanced off my shield. I got the feeling the bullets were hitting harder than the short guns the Black Dog's army used, but even so, the shield would hold so long as I didn't take too many at once.

Then, out of nowhere, the forest opened up before me.

There was a blue sky ahead, and the sun—which had just passed its peak—seared my eyes. I had apparently reached the opposite end of the meager woods. All I could see was a small hill beyond a wasteland with no obstacles in between. Dogs were barking behind me again; they had probably released a new pack. There were more orc roars than before as well. The force from the village had most likely recovered from its confusion and joined the chase.

I would die if I stopped here. It was all or nothing. I took off, sprinting as fast as I could. If I could reach the hill, I wouldn't have to worry about being shot in the back for the time being. If my memories of when I'd flown here served me right, there was a larger forest just beyond it. If I could get there before they reached the hill, perhaps I would be able to shake them off.

Halfway up the hill, everything suddenly went south. Close to a hundred orcs had formed three lines right at the edge of the forest behind me, their guns at the ready. Turning toward the enemy, I deployed a shield of light from both hands and squatted on the spot. They fired, and I angled my shield in the hopes that the bullets would glance off.

A shrill screech pierced my eardrums as my shattered shield let off a flash like blue lightning. A bullet grazed my ear while countless others littered the dirt around me. I could feel my mana rapidly drain away. It took a few seconds for me to recover from the sounds, the lights, and the mana loss. It was evidently a bad idea to pour even more mana in to block the volley.

I made sure Kyel was alive just as a new line of orcs emerged from the smoke. As luck would have it, that barrage came from only one of the three lines. I immediately readied my defenses again. The enemy fired. The shield shattered just as it had before, but the bullets didn't hit me. It seemed the shield angle was paying off. In no time at all, the third line was out in full force. I took a defensive stance with an even greater angle than last time.

Then the third volley hurtled toward me. The shield burst, but I was still in one piece. However, my head was spinning after having my shields broken one after another. I barely managed to move my unsteady feet as I turned my back to the orcs and ran off. Only a few more steps to the summit.

My final leap came at the same time as the sound of guns. A fresh batch of bullets passed over me as I slid headfirst down the slope. I could see a large forest ahead. There was still some way to go, but I was quite a bit faster than the orcs. Once they had finished reloading and reached the hilltop, I would be out of range. For now, it seemed I had surmounted the predicament.

But that didn't mean I could just sit on my laurels. I immediately hoisted myself up and started running. I could only take a deep breath once I was behind those trees. I ran with all my might, but halfway there, I heard that sinister barking from behind.

Woof! Woof! Woof! Woof!

Those hunting dogs again. I glanced back to see ten of them this time. They would catch up before we reached the forest. I tossed Kyel down on the spot and projected a spear from both hands, standing my ground. The dogs surrounded me, not giving Kyel a second glance. I stabbed at the nearest one. It backed off to try to avoid the blow, but now that I had unloaded some weight, I was faster.

First one down.

A second one rushed to its comrade's aid. I took it out with the spear in my other hand. Keeping up that momentum, I cut down one dog after the next. I took out those brave and faithful hounds until not a single one remained, though their courage pained my heart.

I'd taken them down faster than expected. Perhaps I'd reach the forest after all, I thought, getting Kyel back over my shoulder. "Let's go," I said, only to realize that his eyes were fixed on something behind me. The orc soldiers were sprouting from the hill line. I shoved him behind me, formed a shield with both hands, and solidified my defenses.

First shot, done.

Second shot, done.

Third shot, just barely.

I would have a little time before the first line finished reloading. I needed to get as much distance as I could—but with the next step, I toppled sideways.

"H-hero?!"

Kyel untangled himself from me, shielding his broken leg as he propped me up.

"Thanks."

I was back up, preparing for the enemy's gunfire again. I curled up, making myself as small of a target as possible, sticking my hands out, and forming a shield, which fizzled out no sooner than it appeared.

Out of mana.

Kyel's face filled with despair. I formed a spear instead of a shield—though it was only as long as a sword. That was the limit to what I could make now.

With a grin to cheer him up, I said, "It's all right." The despair disappeared from his eyes, but it was replaced with fear. *Why? I was just trying to cheer him up.*

Even so, he pulled a dagger from his waist and readied himself. *Good, that's the spirit. It would be quite a shoddy end, but that's life for you. Why not go out like a hero?*

The sound of a horn interrupted my thoughts.

I turned to see an unbelievable scene. The forest was rustling as horsemen emerged from it. Faced with a sudden cavalry charge, the orcs, who had made it halfway down the hill, fell into a panic, even throwing down the guns they had nearly finished loading. The ground rumbled as the horsemen raced past me with halberds in their hands, trampling down the fleeing orcs.

"Ha... Ha ha ha..."

From the look on his face and the weak laugh, it seemed that Kyel had resolved to meet his death. The sudden miracle had thrown his mind off balance.

⫯✖⫯

After roughly snapping Kyel back to his senses, I lent him a shoulder, and we climbed the hill after the knights who had saved us. We met them at the summit.

"Oh, if it isn't Sir Kyel!" The man in the lead who called out was past his prime with a tanned, scarred face.

"Galeom!" Kyel replied.

"To think we would meet here! Is Rigel in good health?"

"Yes! The same as ever!"

"Splendid! Now then, I'm sure we have much to talk about, but let's head somewhere nicer. Come, get on my horse."

One of the knights got down to help Kyel onto Galeom's horse. Once he was back in his saddle, he pulled me up to sit behind him.

"Now, let's go!" Galeom ordered, and the knights started back toward the forest.

Galeom's camp was set up in the forest's depths. It was rudimentary but had canvas stretched between the trees to ward off the elements. He had forty-seven knights, thirty-eight horses, eighteen foot soldiers, three priests, and three wagons.

We dismounted, and he introduced himself with a bow. "I'm Galeom, son of Armus, and lord of Chezarith Castle." His speech was a bit rough, but his manner was welcoming. "We were charmed by the courage you showed in such dire straits! Such bravery to never abandon your comrade! I would love to get to know you. Please, won't you tell us your name?"

I didn't really mind introducing myself, but would it really be all right to refer to myself here as "the hero summoned to save the world"? That had to sound implausible. He was probably a survivor of the subjugation forces who hadn't answered Liana's summons, so he wouldn't know of me. On the other side of the mountains, I could get the king, or the temple, or Rigel to vouch for me, but without their support, I couldn't introduce myself that way to a complete stranger. At best, I'd be treated like a basket case; at worst, I'd make an enemy of him.

As I hesitated, Kyel stepped up to help.

"Hero, won't you give me the honor of introducing you?"

Good idea. Galeom knew the lad, so there was a much better chance he'd believe the wild story coming from him.

"Please do."

"It would be my honor." He turned back to Galeom. "Are you ready for this, Lord Galeom?"

"Go ahead." Galeom nodded calmly.

"This gentleman is our messiah, the hero whom our priest summoned upon receiving a divine revelation from God!"

His words were met with just the blank stare I had feared. Understandably, of course.

After a moment, Galeom broke the silence. "Hmm. That's hard to believe, but after seeing him cut through a pack of bear-dogs and withstand three volleys of orc fire, I'm forced to believe it."

What, you were watching? You could have helped sooner.

Galeom got down on one knee. "Hero, we must have been brought together by God. I offer my thanks for this meeting." The other knights kneeled as well. For now, at least, it seemed I had their trust.

Lunch was prepared, and as we ate, we began exchanging information.

"When we returned to Dragonjaw after we'd finished our

mission, there was an army of orcs blocking the valley. We were left with no choice but to retreat to orc territory and continue our subjugation," Galeom explained. *Meaning that they ran around plundering food and supplies. Those unfamiliar burn marks I saw must've been his work.*

"Why are you here, Hero?"

I swallowed a mouthful of hard salted meat. "We were burning down orc villages in an attempt to cut off the army in the valley from its supplies and force their retreat. But the orcs were waiting for us, and we were shot down."

I washed the remaining salty grease down with a mouthful of ale. The food was nothing special, but it was flavored with the joy of being alive, and nothing could have tasted better.

"I see," he said. "No wonder I've spotted so many dragons flying around lately. So that was your plan."

He told us that his party generally traveled at night, lurking in the forest during the daylight hours. So that's why we'd never caught sight of him.

"What happened to the orcs in the valley?" he asked me.

"They're still sticking around."

The mood took a turn for the worse. "But if you join us, Hero, it would be as if we gained the strength of a hundred men! The orcs will eventually yield! Until then, we'll have to get by no matter what!"

Galeom's cheerful tone sounded forced—an obvious attempt to dispel the sudden gloom. Kyel and I exchanged a rather awkward look.

"The thing is, one of our riders headed back to inform the others of our survival," I told him. "I presume Rigel will send out a search party tomorrow. We hope to return with their help."

"I see. I know that man, and there is no way he will abandon you. The search party will come without fail. Your safety is assured. No need to look so downcast, Hero."

He let out a grand laugh at my obvious discomfort, but it wasn't my own safety I was thinking of. The envy in the eyes of those around me made me feel ill with guilt. Unfortunately, those without the talent couldn't ride dragons. No matter how they struggled, they weren't all going to make it back.

Once night came, Galeom's men packed up camp without a sound and got ready to move on.

"We can't stay in one place for long," he said. "What are you going to do, Hero?"

I thought for a moment. "I think I'll stay in the area until tomorrow."

"Sounds like a plan. I'll lend you a horse." He chose one and held the reins out to me.

"Oh, no, I couldn't." Relinquishing a horse would be akin to casting aside one of their precious few lifelines. I couldn't take it from them.

Galeom shook his head. "It is not difficult for us to hide for another few days on our own. You need it more. Of course, it's going to cost you, Hero." He handed me a scroll. "Once you return alive, present that letter to my foolish son at Chezarith Castle."

"What is it?"

"There is a coast west of here. Once upon a time, we would use ships to attack the orc fishing villages. These days, it has become difficult to approach them without a horse, so this practice has been lost," he said, looking weary. "In any case, the letter calls for a ship at a designated place on a designated date. It includes a simple sea chart. The point is, if you deliver that, we will be able to return home safely." A grin crept onto his face. "The horse will cost you a fortune, but worry not. The delivery fees are just as hefty in these parts, so it will come out even."

"In that case, I'll gladly borrow it."

We parted with a firm handshake. Under the pale moonlight, a flock of people and horses left in single file.

CHAPTER 7

A DEMON KING IN WHITE

IN THE BARRACKS of the margravate's capital, the chief accountant tossed the notice on the desk with a sigh. It was an elaborately decorated document signed by the supreme commander of the margrave's army.

The chair creaked as he threw himself into it. His glasses slipped down his face as he sagged into a slump, and one of his subordinates—a diligent orc who often found himself scolding his slovenly superior—berated him for his bad posture. In response, the chief nudged his head toward the papers. After glancing over the document, his subordinate looked at him with sympathy in his eyes.

Oh, looks like he actually can *shut up. Nice to see the supreme commander is useful for something.*

Chuckling to himself, the chief accountant gazed out the window. In the yard outside, refugees had gathered in hopes of emergency provisions. The military police struggled to organize the starving masses, who would have killed for food. The margravate was along the northernmost border, and there were refugees every year. The city would always prepare a surplus of food for them, but that didn't seem like it was going to be enough this year. The humans and dragons were running rampant in the north. At the ports, there were more and more refugees knocking on their door.

Just the other day, the mayor had finally come to the margrave in tears. The margrave had immediately ordered for the military's reserves to be offered to the people, thus bringing about this emergency distribution. To the man who ran the army's supply chain, it was a severe headache. The mobilization of the entire army had already been a great burden. If they were to sacrifice their reserves on top of that, it would be difficult to maintain their deployment. This went beyond what was feasible.

On the other hand, they could not simply refuse to provide food. It wasn't only the refugees who were starving. The price of ingredients was rising by the day, and now even the city's original inhabitants were struggling to eat. The starving would do anything for food. That was a threat to public order. At this point, they were on the cusp of rioting.

Additionally, all the soldiers capable of suppressing such a riot had gone out to vanquish the humans. The few remaining military police couldn't possibly handle the situation. The chief accountant knew he would be the first one torn apart, as he had the keys to the army's food storage.

He sighed. He didn't want to be involved in battles—that was the whole reason he'd gone to accounting school. Why was he being exposed to such danger?

So he begrudgingly agreed to offer food, but he also advised the margrave to withdraw his army. Although the margrave hesitated, the accountant managed to convince him with his bank book. The margrave had always been rather sickly and had only grown weaker once he was crushed by his expedition's failings.

Thus, a messenger with a retreat order had been sent off to the expedition force. But his relief was brief. The commander's response read, *"Once my army arrives at the capital, a celebration shall be held for their triumphant return. I leave all of the preparations to you."*

The accountant could not believe his eyes. *A celebration. A* celebration, *he said!* Admittedly, the army had achieved a great victory. They had slain mountains of those vile humans, and their accomplishments were unprecedented. The city had once been ablaze with the news.

But that was before the dragon attacks began.

They were now plagued by hordes of refugees, dwindling food, and the hushed, fearful rumors of dragons. The joy of victory was a thing of the past. Now the majority of the populace was suspicious and resentful of the army because of the lack of aid. So *now* they were supposed to hold a celebration? How would the people forced to flee their burning homes feel about an army marching around, announcing some great victory?

Or maybe that's the idea.

Take that mercenary captain, for instance—the one-eyed hero who rode the black aquilup. A natural-born fighter from a barbarian tribe, he was the guardian of settlers and the true star of their prior victory. Leading the aquilup riders, the noble orc had raced over the open plains, saving any settlement that was in danger. Among the common people—and the soldiers—he was incredibly popular.

With that mercenary at the front of the parade, perhaps the people would be able to remember the feeling of victory, if only for a moment. He wasn't sure if that was what the supreme commander actually intended, but it would be a good way for the people to let off steam.

Am I allowed to decide the order they march in? Of course he was. The document had specified "all of the preparations," after all.

The chief accountant straightened himself and lifted his glasses. He dipped the tip of his pen into his inkwell and began drafting up the orders for the celebration. As he did so, he noticed a small memo in a corner of the envelope the commander's message had come in. A small, unassuming scrap of paper giving off a sinister air. Suddenly nervous, he reached out and unfolded it.

"The barbarian must not participate in the festivities. Keep this a secret from the margrave."

The accountant smacked his pen down on the table. He slouched back down, even deeper than before. Calling his subordinate over, he showed him this new piece of information.

Seeing the bewildered look on the man's face, the chief accountant gave him an order.

"I've got a job for you. Think up an excuse for this."

"Why not convey it as is?" his subordinate replied with an earnest look. "Yes, we could simply relay that the so-called *barbarian* is not to be allowed within the city walls. It's a win for all of us, you see. Once the margrave catches wind of the supreme commander's request, he'll give him a good whipping."

The chief accountant burst out laughing. *Never knew he could make a joke. I'm beginning to think better of him.*

Once he had finally contained himself, he got to work implementing that idea. Then, without lowering his pen, he began drafting his resignation. Naturally, he knew that it would not be accepted. He wasn't a fool. Even so, the way he saw it, he should at least be free to dream about a peaceful retirement.

※

The day after we parted with Galeom, Kyel and I were spotted and picked up by the dragon riders that were dispatched to search for us. Riding double over Dragonbone Ridge was surprisingly terrifying. A normal dragon would be bedridden after carrying just one rider on the return trip. It wasn't hard to imagine what would happen with the additional weight of another adult man.

I probably would have been calmer if I were in control. Having my life depend on someone else's abilities was far scarier than facing an army of orcs. But as the one being saved, I couldn't just tell them to hand me the reins.

When we arrived at the grand dragon house, Rigel ran over to us at full speed, getting down on his knees.

"Hero! I heard you braved great dangers to save our dragon brethren. As captain of the dragon riders, I offer you my utmost gratitude."

"I lost the valuable dragon you lent me. I'm sorry."

"Our fellow riders are more important than dragons. Please don't think about it." Rigel bowed his head and stood. Then, he suddenly turned to Kyel and hammered his fist into his face.

Kyel, who was barely managing to stand with a crutch, was helpless. However, he unsteadily stood back at attention.

"I heard Oifel's report." Rigel glared at him. "Not only did you lose a dragon due to your thoughtless actions, but you exposed the hero to danger. Do you have anything to say for yourself?"

"No, I do not."

"We will have an inquiry another day. Lie low until then."

Rigel pointed at the tunnel of the grand dragon house, and Kyel tottered in that direction along with two other dragon riders.

The old man was angrier than I expected. Perhaps I'd done something wrong. I didn't know what I'd do if Kyel were relieved of his position. I had plenty more work I wanted him to do.

"Rigel, I braved the danger to save him precisely because I see potential in him," I said. "Please don't be too harsh."

For a moment, he looked surprised, but that stern captain's expression quickly returned to his face. "I appreciate the consideration," he said. "However, as a member of the dragon riders, he needs to learn his lesson. Even if the hero expresses support for him, I can't appear to give my grandson special treatment. The resulting rumors would be a serious problem for him."

"My apologies. I shouldn't interfere."

There was a moment of silence.

"Now, then, I'm sure you're tired, Hero," Rigel said. "I have a room and a meal ready for you."

Rigel called an attendant and ordered him to show me the way. We had only gone a few steps when he called me back.

"Hero."

"What is it?"

"Thank you. You brought back my only grandson."

He fell to both knees and covered his face. Not as the captain of the dragon riders but as a grandfather whose grandson was saved, he once again offered his gratitude with sobs in his voice.

"Please, think nothing of it," I said. "I have high hopes for his abilities. I did it for my own reasons."

"Understood! I will definitely retrain him to be a splendid rider who exceeds your expectations!"

The look on his face could only belong to a grandfather. *You should have shown him that face,* I wanted to say. But I decided I wasn't going to stick my nose where it didn't belong. If Kyel wasn't going to be abandoned, there was nothing else I needed to say. My efforts had not been wasted.

I helped Rigel to his feet and let the attendant lead me away. After gulping down a hot meal, I threw myself onto a warm straw mattress. The fatigue reminded me I was alive, and in some strange way, it felt like I had set out just that morning.

Sortie, spotting, cannons, explosions, rescue, falling, dogs, shields, dust, flash, dust, horn.

With the events of the previous day circling around in my head, I was asleep before I knew it.

†|ᛞ|†

It had been a while since I last had that nightmare. My nightmares were all the same. They were about returning from my first world.

"Where did you run off to?!"

No one believed me when I told them I'd saved another world. Of course they didn't. They called me a liar. Only my mother was different. Only my mother believed in me.

My wise mother, however, could tell the difference between believing *in* her dear son and believing what he had to say.

She held my hand on the way to the hospital.

"His memories have been disrupted by intense stress."

"As long as it doesn't affect his ability to function, there is no need to hospitalize him. If you're still worried... Sure. We'll continue his counseling and see where that goes."

She held my hand on the way back home.

But if I denied my memories, I would have nothing left.

I would be nothing.

†|ᛞ|†

It was dim inside the grand dragon house. The light of a flickering torch barely illuminated the caverns built by ancient children. The atmosphere was heavy in the conference room, and not because the torches were burning through our oxygen. Those ancient children hadn't made such a rudimentary mistake. I didn't know how it worked, but there was wonderful air circulation.

I was joined by Rigel and five other veteran riders. It had been three days since we returned from orc territory, and we would need to decide on our policy henceforth.

"First, let's go over the current state of things," said Rigel. "How many dragons do we have left?"

"We've refrained from missions since then, so we currently have twelve ready to fly," reported an old rider with a weary expression on his face.

My Veralgon had just recovered too, though he would need a few more days if I wanted him to fly over those mountains. Just like their riders, dragons simply wouldn't recover if they were pushed too far.

"Even if we send all of them to burn supplies, they won't hold out for three days."

"We'll need to leave a few behind for emergencies and to carry messages."

"The wind above the mountains will get even worse when winter comes. Our recovering dragons might be able to make it across, but they won't make it back."

"I didn't think the enemy would be so thorough with their ambushes. We've already lost three dragons. We can't lose any more."

His brow furrowed, Rigel listened to his men's somber words

as they all voiced their opposition to continuing these operations. They were right, of course. We would be hard-pressed to go on.

At that moment, the youngest of them, who had kept his mouth shut, finally spoke up. "I understand that the situation is fraught with danger. However..." He scanned the faces of the other four. "We've achieved nothing. I see this mission as a battle where the honor of the dragon riders is on the line. If we pull back now, we'll lose all our credibility."

The seasoned riders had no response.

It was Rigel who broke the silence. "Correct. We cannot back down," he said somberly. Everyone focused on him, me included. "I made a promise to the king. If nothing is achieved, our honor will be forever sullied."

I felt like this was all my fault. It was because of my big talk that the dragon riders had to go to such lengths, that they were unable to stop even if they wanted to. I should have been more cautious. I should have said that the plan made no guarantees or that it was my personal opinion.

Suddenly, Rigel smacked the table; the massive disk carved from a single slab of stone trembled beneath his fist. He rose, shouting, "Now that it's come to this, we must send every capable dragon to the enemy camp!"

The veterans were looking at him blankly.

I cried, "Don't be so hasty, Rigel!"

"Don't stop me, Hero! This is all I can do! This is all I have left!" He squeezed out his voice, pressing his clenched fists against the table.

"Stop it! It's pointless!"

I had learned it firsthand while fighting in that village. Considering the state I'd been left in against a mere hundred orcs, ten-odd dragons would only die in vain against ten thousand more.

"If it's pointless, then so be it! If we can no longer stand against the orcs, what reason do we have to exist?! It is a knight's dream to bravely fall before the enemy! We will maintain our honor, even at the cost of our lives! It's the only option."

His eyes were bloodshot. I needed to restrain him somehow.

"Rigel, a frontal assault is not the only way to contribute to a battle. The scouts and messengers make an important contribution that directly influences the outcome. There is no one else who can take on that duty. Please, contain your—"

"But then! Our honor! Is gone! For good! A decisive battle! Is where! We! Must! Die!"

He was getting incredibly worked up. What's more, the old riders who had been against the plan were starting to agree with him. I could see the will to fight flare up in the depths of their tired eyes. It was hopeless.

"Very well. I won't oppose you."

"You finally understand! Well then, everyone! Prepare to charge! I leave the rest to you, Hero!"

"W-wait! I won't stop you, but just wait a bit longer!"

"For what?! I'm always ready to die in battle!"

"Not that. I mean, wait until you have a few more dragons up and running. If you want a most effective attack, wait until everyone has recovered. The dragon riders' honor can only be fully displayed when everyone stands together. The orcs aren't going anywhere."

Rigel groaned. There was a hint of rationality returning to his eyes. Just a tiny hint. But it was a good sign. I didn't know how much time would be needed for all the dragons to recover, but I prayed he would regain his senses by then.

On the other hand, if the dragons recover too fast, that will mean losing all of them. Wait, did I make another mistake? If I let them go now, we'll keep the losses at twelve. But I really don't want Rigel to die for nothing.

At that moment, the door burst open. The man who rushed in was the dragon rider stationed at Dragonjaw Gate for communications. All eyes turned to him.

"I come bearing a report!" he yelled.

He took a moment to collect himself, his shoulders rising and falling with each breath. Everyone waited anxiously for him to recover.

After a deep inhale, he announced, "The orcs have begun their retreat from Dragonjaw Gate!"

Rigel's eyes shot open. "Really?!"

"I saw it with my own eyes! There is no mistaking it! The orcs were leaving the valley one after another."

Still staring, Rigel slowly took his seat. In near disbelief, he asked, "Is it true?"

Seeing the rider's firm nod, he closed his eyes, turned his face to the heavens, and muttered a prayer. We had just received a report of our victory, yet it didn't feel real. The other riders seemed to feel the same way. Not a single one cheered. They simply exchanged looks as if doubting their ears.

Then someone finally let out a sigh, and the atmosphere, stretched so thin with tension, suddenly broke. His prayer finished, Rigel declared that the patrols would continue until they confirmed a complete retreat with their own eyes. Thus, the meeting came to an end.

†|⊠|†

The next day, three other dragon riders and I flew to the valley. The orcs had vastly enhanced their defenses since the last time I saw them. Their palisades snaked around like labyrinths, and, perhaps in fear of the flooding, they had constructed evacuation routes with moats and mounds of dirt. If they'd stayed here, they would definitely have been a problem. In fact, they might have intended to settle there permanently; they had also erected rows of longhouses.

But there was an even bigger difference. The orcs, who had swarmed in unnerving masses last time I was here, had left only a meager rearguard and disappeared. The vastness, might, and majesty of their defenses made the tiny numbers even more striking.

Those remaining soldiers hurriedly gathered the moment they saw the dragons overhead, but such a small force would be no threat so long as we didn't get too close. We let them be and continued our scouting. As we'd discussed, I made sure a dragon was always posted above me before I carefully descended toward the forest. There was a chance they had simply pretended to re-treat and were still lurking in the woods.

I did my rounds low and slow. At times, animals would jump out, spooked by the dragons, but other than that, the forest was quiet and still. Before I realized it, I had reached the edge, and the shadows of the trees were stretching out before me. The sun was already starting to sink. It had been midday by the time we arrived, so this was expected, given the season.

I looked for Rigel, who was also searching the forest. I immediately spotted him on Greilgon, his trusty steed with emerald-green wings. His backup's dragon was black and gold, its wings decorated with a gaudy tiger pattern, the perfect landmark.

I waved at Rigel. After waiting for him to notice and wave back, I signaled for us to return to base. He immediately sig-naled back. With our hands, we let each other know that we'd seen nothing out of the ordinary. The orcs really *were* gone. They weren't in the forest either. We could exchange detailed informa-tion once we returned.

When we touched down at the gate, Herbert gave us a warm welcome.

"As expected of the hero! Your tactics were splendid! To think you really could turn those orcs away with no more than the strength of the dragon riders! You have my admiration!" He hugged me and patted me on the back.

"I only made the suggestion. It is the dragon riders who made it a reality."

I peeled him off of me, and for some reason, the gate garrison who were watching us cheered. Undeterred by my rejection, Herbert turned to Rigel and hugged him too.

"Splendid work, Rigel! You've redeemed yourself! The dragon riders now have a new claim to fame!"

Rigel immediately tried to shake him off but was confused to find that he couldn't. Though he was slight of build, Rigel's muscles had been trained in a way worthy of the captain of the riders. Yet he stood no match against Herbert. I later learned that in his mercenary days, Herbert had been renowned for his monstrous brute strength when swinging around a war hammer. Legend had it that he'd sent eight orcs flying with one swing.

Would the same thing have happened to me if I hadn't possessed my hero's powers? There was no worse way to die than being hugged to death by an old man. I thanked the mysterious entity who'd bestowed these powers upon me.

Herbert finally came to his senses and let Rigel go. And, while Rigel had sweated up a storm in the process, he held out his hand and they exchanged a firm handshake.

"Long live the hero! Our savior!"

"Hail to his name!"

"Glory to the dragon riders!"

"Cheers!"

If the orcs had marched on the gate, the garrison would have been the first to go. Hearing their cheers, I finally realized what had just happened. To me, it was my first victory since I came to this world, albeit a narrow one. To them, it was everything.

A few days after we confirmed the orc army's retreat, Rigel and I were led to the royal audience chamber, where we reported to His Majesty. By then, the orc rearguard had pulled out too, and the mouth of the valley was left completely vacant. Upon hearing this, the boy king lauded our achievements.

"Commendable work. I must say, you did a splendid job driving away such a large army with only meager losses! The dragon riders have renewed their past glory and shown their worth in a new era. No one would dare call you useless anymore. Our nation's strongest shall always be the dragon riders."

"You speak too highly of me, Sire!" Rigel said. "We owe it all to the hero's tactics. We served as no more than his limbs."

Despite his attempt at humility, Rigel's shoulders were shaking in glee. The head of the Knights Templar, who stood by His Majesty's side, looked down at him with a bitter look on his face.

What's that man so angry about? From his expression, you'd think he prefers orcs to Rigel.

The head of the royal guard kept a low profile behind the king but, like His Majesty, looked relieved at the good news. The courtiers also patted their chests in relief. In the corner of the room, that mysterious old man with the sharp eyes stood like a statue, his expression unchanging. Never mind his emotions—I could hardly feel his presence. He was like a seasoned hunter lurking unnoticed by his prey.

His Majesty turned to me.

"As expected of a hero. You're versed in strategy as well as fighting!"

"I am honored by your high praise."

"Incidentally, Hero, would you care to lend me your wisdom and courage one more time?" he asked casually.

"Yes, so long as I can be of some use."

When we met at the reporting ceremony, I had resolved to be of as much use to him as I could. Seeing him do his best to put on a brave act as he shouldered the fate of humanity, who wouldn't feel the same?

I had made a promise to Liana too. Promises to the dead must be honored, no matter the world.

"As field marshal, I want you to end a territory dispute."

Ugh. Despite my resolve, that was definitely going to be a pain. *Maybe I can find a way out of this...*

"Your Majesty, when you appointed me to my position, you told me to do my best not to get involved in any human conflicts. I am from another world—an outsider. If possible, I would like to stick to my initial policy."

I'd somehow thrown together a totally plausible rationalization, but he immediately saw the flaw in it.

"It's a bit late for that," he replied. "I heard you brought quite a skillful end to the conflict in Morsharz. Without notifying me, at that."

Okay, but I didn't get involved because I wanted to. I was dragged into it.

"I can only say that the matter was a pure coincidence," I said.

"Luckily, those involved did not wish for conflict. The peace was achieved not by my power but by God's design." It would be too pathetic to say I was strung along by a woman, so I blamed it on God. *He can't argue with that, can he?*

He could. "Then that makes the hero an agent of God's will. I can think of no one better to suppress the conflicts."

The king was making me out to be a messenger of God. No, I guess that was my original setting? As I racked my brains for some clever retort, His Majesty continued on with the same buoyant attitude. "No need to worry, the war has already been settled. All you need to do is show your face."

"What do you mean it's settled?"

What am I supposed to do, then?

"You are to clean up afterward. If I make you the agent of authority, then the victor can wield their power, and the losers will have an excuse to accept their losses. The peace treaties have already been established; all that remains is for my proxy to sit at their signing."

I see. Then it wouldn't be too much trouble after all.

"Very well," I said. "Then I shall put an end to these unproductive quarrels in Your Majesty's name. Incidentally, what region will I be suppressing?"

"Kerulgarz."

Where had I heard that name before?

"What are you playing dumb for? Kerulgarz is just south of your own territory."

And so, I was shipped off to Kerulgarz, a land devastated by civil war.

The Black Dog arrived at the orc settlement east of Dragonbone Ridge two days after the dragon attack. He had made haste with his aquilup riders the moment he saw the signal.

It was impossible to station a defensive force capable of fending off the dragons at every village, but if he sent an army only after the dragon appeared, they would never make it in time. Reluctantly, he was forced to station troops at a select few villages and wait for the enemy to fall for the trap.

One of them finally fell for it. The one who came out to meet the Black Dog was an officer in training, still at the age where he was more boy than man. By his word, the commander died during the attack, and he, the only remaining officer, took command. Half of the troops were lost, while two valuable cannons went up in flames. The losses were great—there was no getting around that. Losing the cannons was especially painful. While they were from an older generation, the margrave's army did not have many of them to spare.

Despite this, the officer trainee stuck out his chest and declared, "Even so, we managed to take out three dragons!"

That certainly was extraordinary enough to make up for their losses. Over the course of the last month, many villages had been burned to the ground by the dragon attacks. They had finally managed to turn the tables on them for once. Considering the situation in the margrave's capital, it was an important accomplishment. An intense dissatisfaction was building against the army's failure to do anything about the dragons—so said the report from the chief accountant. If they could report that they had managed to slay some of those vile dragons, they would be able to regain some of the people's trust.

The Black Dog pressed for more details. One dragon was felled by a surprise shot from the cannons. A counterattack from the moss-green dragon then managed to take both cannons out. One swooped down to save its comrade and was shot dead.

Meanwhile, a counterattack from the remaining two dragons sent the formation into disarray and disrupted the line of command. One of the dragons tried to use the chance to save its comrade, only to run into soldiers who were there by coincidence. It was nothing but good news so far.

However, while chasing the dragon's escaped rider, they collided with an armored cavalry that had appeared out of nowhere. Most of the casualties occurred then, including the death of their commander. The trainee had been in command ever since, setting up palisades and awaiting reinforcements.

There was nothing else they could do. The cavalry numbered around thirty. When the humans had their shamans with them, it would take a hundred guns to beat them. In fact, it was impressive that the youngster had managed to maintain his unit for so long. He had promise, there was no doubt about that. The Black Dog asked for his name again and carved it into his heart.

The escaped dragon rider had already left with the cavalry. The next day, multiple dragons were spotted on patrol, not launching any attacks. They were presumably there to pick up the rider.

There was no use staying around here. The Black Dog made his decision to withdraw the army and make straight for the capital without reuniting with the main force. The margrave's army at the mouth of the valley had received a retreat order just the other day. The refugees flooding into the city were putting a strain on its food supply, meaning that the margrave had no reserves left for the army. It had become too difficult to maintain their deployment.

The trainee relayed the orders to the soldiers by his side, sending them off to convey them to the rest of the garrison. He turned to the Black Dog, his puffed nostrils indicating he had something more to say, but he instead turned back to return to his men.

The Black Dog stopped him and asked what he wanted to say.

After a moment's hesitation, the youngster began, "You might not believe me, but..." He went on to explain that one of the dragon riders was a terrifying monster who raced as fast as a cat even while shouldering his wounded comrade. With his spear, he'd cut down more than twenty bear-dogs, and he had projected shield after shield, fending off volleys of fire from a hundred guns.

The story was ludicrous. No wonder he'd hesitated to report it. Normally, if anyone made such a nonsensical report, their sanity would be called into question. They would say the young trainee had gone mad, his mind broken by the stress.

The Black Dog didn't think so. He had an idea of who the trainee was talking about. It was that man, there was no doubt about it. The monster who wounded him had shown up again. His wound throbbed. When he put a hand to his flank, it was still oozing blood.

He heard out the report in full, pondering over each detail.

The dragon attacks this time were barbaric. There was no plunder involved—their sole objective was pure destruction. That was unique in his experience of the humans. By first giving a warning, the enemy had essentially created refugees. Perhaps there was a method to the man's madness, but more than anything, it suggested a bottomless malice. This was no doubt his work.

He would need to give a name to that unique entity. Now, what would he call him?

The young man concluded, "It was almost like he was the Great Demon King of legend."

Demon King. He who commanded legions of demons. A cruel, peerless, vile king. The symbol of fear featured in so many legends. *Indeed, it was a fitting name,* the Black Dog thought with a ferocious smile. In the stories, the Demon King was slain without fail.

MY FIRST WORLD:
MEETING THE WATER PRIESTESS

WHEN I LOOKED at the clock, the hands were pointing to midnight on the dot. I set down my book and stretched out.

My desk was occupied by a notebook and a set of math problems. I had drawn, erased, and redrawn so many auxiliary lines over the proof I'd copied down that it had become completely incomprehensible. There was a cup of tepid hot cocoa in the corner. My mother had made it to encourage me in my studies, and my guilt over slacking off to read rather than study prevented me from touching it, leaving it to go cold. It felt wrong to throw it out. I downed it in one gulp. The gritty texture that had settled at the bottom made my guilt even worse.

Even if I wanted to start studying again, there was little point in doing it today. Surely, the risk of ruining my health by staying up outweighed any benefit a few extra hours of studying could provide. Once I reached that epiphany, I closed the notebook and problem set, shoving both into the shelf by my desk. I didn't have any reason to study so hard to begin with. I'd taken my grades into consideration when picking the school I was testing for—even my teacher had said I was all set to pass.

Yet when it came down to it, I didn't have the courage to sit around doing nothing, nor did I have the motivation to throw myself into pointless preparations. So I was left wasting day after day on half-baked measures. It was a real drag.

Once my writing supplies were put away, I found my hand reaching out for the novel I'd been reading. Only ten pages left. Why not finish it before going to sleep? That would certainly give me more motivation for the next day.

The book was one where a young boy summoned to another world accomplished great feats with the immense powers granted to him by a beautiful goddess. I'd already read it a number of times. I knew every development from beginning to end, and while they didn't excite me by this point, it didn't sit right with me to leave it half-finished. I read the last few pages in no time, then set the book to the side and took a big stretch.

Why can't something like that happen to me? I thought. And the moment I did, I felt the backrest of my chair disappear and my body toppling backward.

᛫ᛉ᛫

Somehow, I'd tumbled into some water. I didn't remember hitting the surface, but the moment I opened my mouth to cry out, a large volume of water suddenly rushed in and sent me into a panic. I flailed my arms, not knowing which way was up, quickly brushing up against what I assumed to be the bottom. With that point of reference, I lifted myself up somehow or other. Now that I was sitting up and calming down, I realized the water only reached to my knees.

What was the meaning of this? Why was I naked?

Just then, I heard a splash.

I looked up and came face-to-face with a naked girl, collapsed on her behind, like I was on mine. Her eyes were wide open, her mouth flapping wordlessly. I didn't know where I was, but this could be an extremely problematic situation. What if the girl screamed? What if someone heard her, raced in, and got the wrong idea? I needed to calm her down, fast. First, I would have to explain the situation... Except I hadn't the slightest idea. Why *was* I here? My thoughts were flying all over the place.

I got to my feet but then suddenly remembered I was buck naked. The girl was staring at me as I presented myself. It was hopeless. Who in their right mind would hear out my excuses?

"Oh... Oh..."

A faint, lovely voice leaked from her lips. She was on the verge of recovering from her initial shock. No doubt she would make a loud noise soon. Just my luck. I had to get away.

I turned, only to find an enormous stone statue blocking my path. It had a long horse-like face over an emaciated body with pronounced ribs. Six fragile, gnarled arms extended from each side, as if to catch me right in the act. To the left and right, I was surrounded by walls. The only exit had to be...

"Oh, dear God..."

I heard a voice from behind. She was finally coherent. I made my resolve to confront her. For some reason, she was tearing up as she looked at my face. Even more perplexingly, there was relief in her expression. On her knees, she shambled up to me, looking up to me with her hands in prayer.

"Please, please save us. Save the world."

What was she talking about? I was the furthest thing from God, but when I saw the look in her eyes, I couldn't say no.

Let your imagination take flight with Seven Seas' light novel imprint: Airship